WE ARE GHOSTS, AFRAID TO WAKE UP

BY

Dakota Snaketail

PART ONE

SLEEP

Static, a hum that puts you to sleep. Someone cries, a ripped piece of paper in a broken typewriter, a sleeping kitten.

LISTEN: _____ ____ __ _ _____.

A flash of light across the sky and Avery dies. He wanted to die because of a comet in his sleep, with a half-lit cigarette still between two fingers that hung off the left side of the bed. His typewriter, that had sat on his desk for the past three years, still had a half-finished story in it. The old woman who lived next door woke up crying. Avery had never bothered to learn her name. The kitten mews and licks Avery's cold, blue face. The bottom of a ghost's coat slips through the door a second before it closes. It knows nothing, it's just a nameless thief.

....

It's three-thirty in the morning, the stars will still be out for a little while. Avery shuts off an alarm and stares at the ceiling.

STARES,STARES,STARES,STARS,STARES.

He finally rubs his eyes, throws a black blanket off his tall, lanky body and sits up. He reaches for a pair of glasses on the end table and puts them on. They sit lopsided on his face. He gets off the bed and stretches. A kitten named GOD rubs up against his leg in their traditional morning routine. The kitten follows Avery out of the bedroom, through a dark hallway, and into the kitchen. Avery flips a switch and waits, listening to the hum of a single, uncovered fluorescent light bulb warming up into light. GOD waits patiently by two empty silver bowls that sit on the floor next to the refrigerator. Avery fills GOD's water bowl and then a coffee pot with lukewarm tap water. GOD feverishly jumps at the water while Avery struggles to set the bowl down without spilling any on the filthy linoleum floor.

GOD stops drinking and walks to the empty space where his food bowl goes and waits for Avery to set the bowl down. Avery quietly laughs to himself in the dry way people do when they haven't spoken in a few days, and grabs a bag of coffee. He pours too much into a white filter and turns the machine on. He sits on the counter between a dirty microwave and a dirty sink, and watches GOD eat while listening to the bubbling noises coming from the coffee maker. He twists his body to reach into a door less cupboard for his favorite yellow mug. GOD jumps to join him on the counter and sits on his pajama covered lap. Avery pets the kitten and softly tells him about last night's dreams. Avery has no way of knowing, but the kitten loves it when Avery describes his dreams.

Steam from the coffee pot burns Avery's arm and he almost drops GOD when he jumps off the counter. He opens the dirty refrigerator door and peers into it, looking for a half-empty bottle of cheap creamer. He grabs it and a packet of sugar from another door less cupboard. He breathes in the smell of the creamer mixing with the coffee and then takes a delicate sip. He reaches into the pocket of his pajama pants and takes out a crumpled, slept-on pack of cigarettes. He lifts GOD into the crook of his arm, turns off the kitchen light, walks into the living room, and pulls the toggle of a dirty lamp. He sits on an old, dirty sofa and sets his mug on a half-broken table in front of him. GOD squirms out of his grip and lays down on an arm rest.

Avery looks at the cat with a sad smile.

"There's supposed to be a meteor shower tonight, GOD. What do you think about that?"

The cat looks up at him and mews a response to Avery. Avery doesn't know, but the cat just told him that he doesn't like meteor showers, that they scare him like the thunderstorms do. Avery obliviously smiles, nods, and takes a drag from his cigarette. He gets up, goes to the dust caked window and looks outside through a smeared circle. It has been snowing. He thinks to himself, 'I wonder if this is what death ever looks like?'

(It is.)

Avery closes the curtain and walks back to the sofa, bumping his knee on the coffee table. He isn't sure, but he thinks he doesn't have work today. *(He does.)* He won't go in regardless. He leans back and turns on the television. He turns to a news channel and falls back asleep.

....

It's eleven in the morning, and Avery jerks awake. He looks around for GOD, but he's in the bathroom, licking Avery's toothbrush. Avery takes a sip from his coffee mug, but spits the cold coffee back into the cup. He walks to the kitchen, pours out the old cup into the sink and makes himself a new cup from the pot he had forgotten to turn off. His phone rings from the bedroom, but he ignores it. 'It's probably just someone from work', he says to himself. Walking back to the couch, he lights himself another cigarette. He stops just in front of the couch, then walks to the window and looks outside again. It has snowed more. It's still what death sometimes looks like to a living being, if that living being wasn't living anymore. Avery turns around and GOD is back on his arm rest of the couch, staring.

STARING,STARING,STARING.

He scratches the cat's ears and looks at the static ridden television screen. He watches the reporter talk about something he doesn't give a shit about, like a mass murder or a cult suicide, something like that. Avery takes a drag of his cigarette, chokes on the stale and unlit taste, and throws it into an overflowing ashtray. He gets up and walks into his bedroom. He reaches for the end table where his glasses had rested and turns on another dirty lamp. The dust on lamp shade casts strange shadows on the barren, off-white walls. The rack where his clothes hang is in the darkest corner of the room, and Avery stands looking towards it. Slowly, he gets naked walks to the rack. He deliberately looks at each article of clothing intently before choosing what to wear.

He gets dressed: A white button shirt with a paint stain on the left cuff, a red tie, a pair of bleach stained boxers, a pair of deep grey slacks that are torn just above his right knee, grey wool socks, brown Oxford loafers, and a dark grey pea coat. He turns away from the rack of clothes and walks towards a pile of them on the floor. He kneels and sifts through it. Finally, he finds what he was looking for: A pair of black winter gloves and a brown wool cap.

Avery turns off the lamp and walks back into the living room. He scratches the cat again, and tells him goodbye, that he'll be back in a little bit. GOD purrs, telling him to have a good walk, enjoy himself and the fresh air. He cares. "He's the only ones," Avery says softly with a sigh. He goes into the kitchen, turns off the coffee maker and the light, then walks out the front door, locking it behind him. The hallway is dimly lit, but Avery prefers it like that. Bright lights always make him sick to his stomach and his head hurt. He walks toward the building door, taking a deep breath before stepping outside, into winter and the unwant(ing)ed world. He looks around, deciding which way to walk. He walks left, looking up at the grey, cloudy sky; his breath fogging up his glasses. There are black birds chirping at a squirrel beneath them. Avery stops and watches the debate before continuing into the parking lot of the apartment complex. He buttons up his coat and wishes that he had a scarf. He walks until he reaches a hole in a chain-link fence big enough for him. He climbs through the hole and slips on a patch of ice.

"SHIT!"

There is a school nearby and there are the sounds of children's playing. Avery walks in the direction of the school, looking at the patches of snow that have remain untouched by the feet of children. 'Children always ruin the sanity of freshly fallen snow.' Avery follows boot prints to a hill where the children are sledding. There is a boulder nearby, so he brushes the snow off it and sits down. As he watches the kids, he remembers something from when he was young.

(("Mom, you said you would take me sledding)))

((today!"))

(("I know what I said, but I have to work."))

((Mother is putting her coat on and leaving))

((me at home by myself because she couldn't))

((get a sitter. She's leaving the television))

(((on so I can watch the Saturday morning))))

((cartoons, but I read my books instead. She))

((says that books are a waste of time, but I don't)

((((think that they are. Someday, I'll be a)))

(((writer.))

(() A snowball hits Avery's foot and he comes back to the present. There is a little girl standing a few feet away smiling at him, her gloves are covered in snow. When he smiles back, she giggles and runs away. Back to her friends she runs, and they huddle together, talking and watching him. He waves at them, and they giggle again.

He gets up and walks down the hill, almost getting hit by a run-away toboggan that escaped tiny hands. He walks towards a wooded area, to get away from the children, back to the sanity of untouched snow. He listens to the wind shaking the dead limbs of the trees, causing big chunks of snow to fall off them. The snow lands on the ground with soft 'THUD's. He listens to the birds and the squirrels and the rabbits and the wind. To him, it's all music. To him, it's a story that has been written countless times, but has never actually been written at all. Someday, he'll use that old typewriter on his desk to finish that story, he thinks. Maybe, he'll do it when he gets back home. He is not motivated these days. Everything seems pointless to him. He thinks there is no point, no one wants to read what he writes, no one wants to hear what he doesn't really have to say. *(He's right.)*

Somehow, he's walked in a circle. He's walked back to his apartment building without realizing it. He opens the door with numb hands, and walks down the dimly lit hallway to his door. 23A. He unlocks the door and walks inside. GOD is sitting at the door waiting for Avery to tell him about his walk. He meows: "Hello, Avery! How was your walk?" Avery asks him what time it is, looking at the clock on the hallway wall. It's four in the afternoon. Avery sits on the floor by GOD and kisses his head. "I think I had a good walk, it's nice to take time to think," Avery says, half to himself and half to the cat. GOD loves Avery's voice and rubs his face on Avery's still gloved hand to show him so. Avery takes off his glove so that GOD can feel his cold, blue hand.

Avery gets up and walks to his bedroom, grabs his typewriter and takes it to the living room in the dark. He opens the curtain covering the window and sets the typewriter on the coffee table. He goes to the kitchen and makes another pot of coffee. When it's done, he takes his steaming mug to the living room and starts writing. It's part suicide note and part letter to someone who left him months ago..

"

"

"

"""""""""""""""""".......

The cats make their food bowls

clank.

Another pot of coffee

*and four more cigarettes. Flip the vinyl
record again. When I feel abandoned*

*all I can think of is abandoning someone
else, even if I wasn't actually*

*abandoned. Even if I was the one who had
abandoned. I feel lost, so I ask myself an old
question, a paraphrase of someone else's
question:*

Go to work

or

commit

suicide

?

She called us "the Fox and the Owl". We dug a hole, or buried our beaks in our chests when it got too cold, or too hard to live, or when we ran out of cigarettes. We all die, I just want to go before all my friends(turnouttonotbefriendsatall).

They laughed.

I don't doubt someone, somewhere will miss me; but why should I care? I'm a selfish, toxic asshole, remember? Will you miss me? I wouldn't, if I were you, you get all my things when I go.

When I go, I'll write and tell you what

happens there... Where ever "there" is....

Flip the vinyl record again. Another cup of coffee and three more cigarettes.

Listen: I want to go. If I paid someone to kill me, would I still be selfish? (Of course.)

Listen: She's already left you mentaly. You're alone mentallly, asshole. (Misspelled life.)

I choke on saliva and blood. Flip the record again.

((IT'S BROKE, AND DON'T ANSWER THE PHONE))

"

"

"

When he finishes, he leans back in the sofa and thinks about throwing it away, but he's too cold. Too apathetic. He looks at the television and realizes he forgot to turn it off. He leans forward and put an elbow on his knee. He winces. He forgot about bumping his knee earlier. He leans back again, half watching the news, half watching GOD play with a loose thread from the carpet. He laughs, and GOD stops. He slowly walks over to Avery and climbs onto his lap. They both fall asleep and dream of the same thing.

A Broken Galaxie.

With Broken stars.

A Broken Galaxie with Broken

people.

A Broken Galaxy with Broken

cats.

Avery wakes up to GOD licking his face. He gets up and puts more food and water into GOD's bowls and makes himself another cup of coffee. Avery stands, leaning against the counter and watches GOD eat. Every few bites, GOD will stop to lick his lips and to look at Avery. Avery lights a cigarette and asks GOD if he'd like one, but he politely refuses.

It's nine forty-five at night. There is a knock at the door and Avery opens it. A ghost named Hope walks in and says hello. GOD stays in the kitchen and meows. He doesn't like the and is telling it to leave. Neither Avery nor the ghost have any way of knowing that. The two humans sit on the couch and have an awkward, forced conversation. Eventually the ghost starts to take off its clothes, still talking. Avery doesn't listen, he starts typing

again...
....

"

"

"

"""""""""""""""""".......

I AM SAD

BECAUSE I CAN'T DRILL

HOLES

THROUGH MY FINGERS

OR POKE STRING THROUGH

THEM

AND ENTANGLE MYSELF

LIKE

A PUPPET.

I CAN STARE

LIKE A MANNIKIN

BUT I THINK

THEREFOR IM

NOT STILL ENOUGH

TO MAKE MONEY

AT BEING SOMEONES

PUPPET OR

DUMMY.

((S. PAUL))

(I DIDENT KILL HER!)

"

"

"

The ghost takes Avery's hand and leads him to the bedroom. They sit on the bed in the dark and Avery opens a drawer in the end table. He takes out a bottle and pours the pills into his mouth without the ghost seeing. They fuck, and the ghost feels nothing. They fuck, and he feels nothing. Even when Avery cums, he still feels nothing. They lay on the bed, side by side, feeling nothing. The ghost tells Avery that its name really isn't Hope. He doesn't ask it what its real name is, he decides to keep it nameless. He gets off the bed to bring his typewriter back into his room and sets it gingerly back on the desk. He lights a cigarette and lays back down on the bed, over the covers to distance himself from the ghost. They fall asleep.

A flash of light and Avery dies. He wanted the comets to hit him while he slept, a half-lit cigarette still between two fingers hanging off the left side of the bed, a burn mark in the carpet. His typewriter, which had sat on his desk for the past three years, until today, still had a half-finished story in it. The old woman who lived next door woke up crying. Avery had never bother to learn her name. The kitten meows and licks Avery's cold, blue face. The bottom of a ghost's coat slips through the front door, seconds before it closes. It knows nothing, it's a nameless thief.

(Everything is white.)

A flash of light across the sky and GOD wakes up. He was sitting on his arm rest of the sofa. He whimpers, crying out for Avery. GOD runs into the kitchen, sniffing the coffee pot to see if it's fresh. It's not, it's cold. He turns, jumps off the dirty counter, and runs to the bathroom. Avery isn't in there either. "Did he go for another walk?", GOD asks himself over and over. Finally, he peers into the bedroom and sees a strange light staring at Avery's motionless body on the bed.

STARING,STARING,STARING.

The ghost looks at GOD, it's makeup is faded and runny from tears. It hurriedly gets dressed and rushes out of the room, out of the apartment. It almost trips over GOD on it's way out. He ignores the ghost and jumps onto the bed. He licks Avery's face, saying, "Wake up! Wake up! WAKE UP! WAKE UUUUUUUUUUUUUUUUUUUUUUPPPPPPPPPPP!" If GOD could cry, he would. "Not... My... Avery...."

(Everything is white.)

Somewhere, in West Oregon, a man wakes up, covered in a cold sweat which makes his skin feel like ectoplasm. He has tears streaming down his fat, red cheeks. He lights a cigarette and turns in his queen-sized bed to his beautiful wife sleeping next to him. He gently shakes her with the hand that isn't holding the cigarette. (He doesn't want to burn her.) She wakes up with an unattractive snort, meant as an answer to him shaking her.

"I just dreamt I was a cat, named GOD, and my master killed himself after screwing a ghost. It was the worst fucking feeling I've ever experienced! It was fucking horrible. What do you suppose it meant?"

"NOTHING."

"NOTHING."

"Nothing."

"Nothing."

"nothing."

"nothi

....

STATIC

(Everything seems normal in a dream.)

SLEEP.
THUNDER.
THUNDER.
THUNDER.

I will let the lightning's static pierce my fingertips while I sleep. There are rocks above my bed that are supposed to keep nightmares, but instead, they keep away <u>all</u> my dreams. I wake up crying, not remembering a single dream.
I lay down in bed, binaural beats coming through headphones, unnatural melatonin slowly creeping through my bloodstream towards my brain. *(It doesn't make any on*

its own.) Creatures walk through the bedroom door and surround the bed. They have long black robes and no face, only bright lights shining from under their lifted hoods. It feels like a dream, but I can feel closest creature's robe brushing against my arm, a static shock. I can't open my eyes or move, but I can see they've transported me somewhere new. I can see them through my eyelids, they are staring down at me.

STARING,STARING,STARRY,STARING. I can see them and myself, simultaneously looking through my eyelids and looking from a floating spot above us. I'm lying on my bed, but I am no longer in my room. Everything is white around us, and the white surrounds and goes on forever into infinity. The closest creature to me touches my forehead and I get a static shock. Everything becomes

STA"""

ııı
ııı
ııı
ııı
ııı
ııı
ııııııııııııııııııııııııııııııııııııı

I'm in a car going down an empty highway at night, the car littered with empty coffee cups and cigarette packs. The highway is empty except for all the ghosts I'm driving through. I recognize one every few miles: An author, and actress, and ex-president. They just float and stare at me while the car goes through them under all the bright stars and planets.

STARE,STARE,STARE,STARS,STARE.
I can't tell how long I've been in this car, but considering all the trash that keeps catching on fire, it's been awhile. The last thing I

remember was crawling through and old television, a looking glass television.

I look down at my hands and they're covered in blood, small pin-pricks of the stuff, like I hit glass. 'Maybe, it's from the television', the radio tells me. 'That's not a bad idea', I say to myself.

I look out the windshield and it's raining. Another mile marker passes, but it says '1', just like the other thousand or so markers I've gone past in the last thirty seconds. There is thunder, and a flash of lightning static goes painlessly through my fingertips. I open a pack of cigarettes, take one out, light it, and roll down the window. I breathe the smoke in deep, and as I exhale, I stick my head out the window and look into the car's side mirror. My eyes are black and bleeding. I touch my cheeks but there is no blood on my hand when I pull it away. I look back into the mirror again and my face appears as a large black dog's face, then goes back to normal with my black and bleeding eyes.

A drop of blood falls on my lap and I look up. The ceiling of the car is bleeding and I see my own ghost crying. His/her ectoplasm dips into my skin. It feels sweet and smells sticky. There is a note nailed to the throat of my ghost, but I can't understand the writing. The ghosts speak:

"(There is static in these worlds. You are not safe. This is the Valley of
Soft Pink. You are safe. Can you hear the color?
Coming from purple lightning? It says you are dreaming, but I say you are not. Black and bleeding is normal. The dog is not. Your cigarette has gone out and relit itself five times already. There is a song playing in some other world, it goes like this:

Do you hear it? It may sound like static, But there are a thousand and two and three-quarter voices singing half a word at the same time for infinity. You cry blood because it's beautiful.)"

I cry blood because the STA".".".".".".".TIC is beautiful. I look at the driver's seat. There is no one at the wheel. I look at the windshield. Static lightning pierces my fingertips painlessly and the highway ends. The ghosts separate, the car and my black and bleeding eyes go off a cliff. The sun comes up and everything becomes static.

....

I

DREAM

OF

A

BABY

DREAMING

OF

WHALES

SHE'S

NEVER

SEEN

(everythingbecomesstatic.)

....

Thirty minutes of static coming from a broken boombox on a broken white desk in a broken white room in a broken black Galaxie Deluxe. I sit in a chair, my arms are bleeding, but you can call it "art" if it makes you feel better. If it makes you feel less guilty. I think I jerk awake but I'm still in a broken chair in a broken room in a broken black Galaxie Exuled.

BROKEN, BROKEN, EVERYTHING IS

ALWAYS FUCKING BROKEN HERE.

I sit and think while I bleed: 'I suppose this could be a life once more, where the audience barely whispers "HELLO". Sucking on nicotine and the forest wind just sleeping on me. Living in a broken cabin made of rotting wood and a broken cabinet filled with coffee just waiting to be brewed. A child climbing on an over-excited apple tree. I'll write stories, some with static sound and some with broken wo rds. I'll move somewhere where it almost always rains. The air will smell like pine needle and river water. The air will feel like ectoplasm on my skin. An empty picture frame that plays movies without a sound, except for mine.' *I'm fighting sleep, you know.* The static from the boombox envelopes everything.

....

I slept in a dingy apartment with three cats waiting for the typewriter to come alive and start typing something for me, while someone who looks like Audrey Hepburn stares at me from five different places in the *((I apologize for the wait, the ink ribbon ran its end and asked to be rewound and a cigarette asked to be smoked))* room.

     STARES,STARES,STARES,STARES.
I slept to the static sounds of tapping, it wrapped its salty fingers around me like a ripped-up blanket. Someone plays the same three notes on violins, three dingy apartments down from mine, static screeching and tapping the whole time. I slip into another dream (everything becomes static).

    ....

I take another sip of coffee and look around the diner. The ghosts I'm with are saying something, but I have things on my mind, so many other things to the point that I can't comprehend what it is their broken vo ices are saying with their stupid and ugly mouths. They each have an untouched sandwich in front of them and they've probably had too much to drink. I'm not hungry. I'm just bored, so I keep drinking coffee.

One, two, three cups.

I can already tell there will be more before I leave, and the waitress comes up to the booth for the fourth time.

"You folks still doing okay? You want another cup of coffee?" The waitress' loud fucking voice permeates into the spell I had put myself under and I jump when she speaks.

"Um. yeah, I'll another, please. Thanks." I say it with a forced smile, hoping it doesn't seem to forced or rude. *(Fuck it.)* Oh well. The waitress walks away, and I pour the contents of a pink sugar packet and a creamer into the fresh coffee. The tinkling of the spoon against the mug mixes with the tinkling of other dishes being washed in the kitchen and the few other groups eating loudly at this ungodly hour. I watch the two ghosts on the other side of the booth talking, to each other and to me *(I think)*, but I can't hear them, so I just smile. *(Again, forced.)* I can only hear the clinking and tinkling of glass dishes and the cars driving past the windows. The headlights from the passing cars go through the partially opened blinds and make streaks of light race across the inside of the diner. The hanging light fixtures that are inside this place slowly sway in circles from the air conditioning system. I tilt my head back and stare at them while they dance, hot coffee burning the inside of my mouth.

STARE,STARE,STARE,STARE,STARE. The two ghosts across the booth, Ellie and Alex *(I think)*, are still talking. they are starting to get louder, so I have no choice but to listen in on their conversation. Ellie, the younger looking one, is asking if I have ever been a vegetarian. I tell it, "Yes, a long time ago." They go back to talking to each other, quieter. I watch them talking and stab a steak knife into my left hand, dropping the coffee cup. With a loud crash, it breaks on the floor. No one notices a thing. There is no blood coming from the stab wound in my hand, only ectoplasm seeps out of the gash and it floats towards my ghost's gaping static mouth on the ceiling.

....

There is a giant monster with dreaded and dirty hair. Its breath feels sweet and sticky on my neck and smells stickier and sweeter. It is chasing me through a canyon, a bright red and purple and orange canyon. I'm tired from running and I trip on a rock. The monster looms over me while I cry bloody on the dusty ground. It reaches down with a long and mold covered claw. It rips through my throat and everything becomes static.

....

I'm clambering around on all fours, running my hands through a creme colored carpet, searching for bits of fallen tobacco. The slightly broken fan is pushing hot air onto my back and it's making a click, click, CLICKing sound with each rotation. The room smells like burnt apple pie and it's murky as hell. The soft red cushions that used to circle the blood stain have been thrown around the room in every direction as I feebly search the carpet, the off-white walls look dark grey through the smoke and I choke a little with each breath. If I open my eyes for too long, they start to burn. I wonder why the lone fire alarm in my apartment hasn't gone off yet.

I get off the floor and walk to the closet, I open the door and I can see the vastness of space and a bright red and purple and orange nebula. The flames that are swallowing my apartment start to burn my back. I step out into the nebula and everything becomes static.

......

"Step outside,
Step outside from that blood-stained bathroom.
You won't look in the mirror,
With all that regret you exhume.
Walk through your halls with the end drawing near.

Step outside,
Step outside and they've heard the gun shots.
They'll look to you for answers,
You know the look up to you in their own dreams

*Because you're the only one of the Beggars
With something they'll never have, and you
know it.*

*Step outside,
Step outside and don't let your horror show.
As soon as they know,
They'll drag you under for betraying him.
They'll throw you in a fire of amber,
You've got no safety net now.*

*You'll die now,
Awfully,
In the cold snow."*

My ghost sings these broken wo rds. It's almost time to wake up. It's almost time to leave this place. The static is almost gone. The static is almost gone. My ghost is always making noises and when we sleep, the noises slip onto our skin and it feels like ectoplasm. Once again, everything turns to static.

....

What is this? The fifth or sixth night I've spent watching the moon roll past the horizon? Not changing clothes, which reek of forgotten dreams and ectoplasm. All I know is that there's been a blizzard outside for the past week. My best friend and I haven't even been able to walk down the street to the gas station to buy cigarettes. Luckily, we opted to buy a carton right before the unexpected blizzard hit. No one, especially us, knew the blizzard was coming, we just realized we had never bought a carton before and thought, 'Why the hell not?' No time like the present, or something.

It's been a nice change of pace, listening to the wind and snow smack the windows and read instead of going to work. Read, or watch movies, or play Monopoly, which gets real fucking boring real fucking quick, so it's a good thing we have two other options. Plus, we've gotten pseudo-philosophical over the past few days, as a result of our seclusion and a bag of blood, so we always have something or another to talk about.

But right now, I can't sleep *(Again.)*, and I shot a ghost in his bed twenty minutes ago. I'll never understand how easy it is for things to fall asleep. But, I've got a hunch no one else in our complex is awake either because there isn't a single light coming from any windows. Right now, everything has an orange glow from the soft, hazy light coming from a few street lamps reflecting off the snow. The only other light is coming from a traffic light a few blocks away and I can't even see that when the snow falls just hard enough. I've watched the lights change every night the blizzards been calm enough to let me see them and it hasn't bored me yet because they always look a little different through the falling snow.

(RED,YELLOW,GREEN: ALL THROUGH STATIC SNOW.)

It's always been my favorite thing about blizzards: the way the lights reflect off the snow and it makes it look like sunrise when it's only two o'clock in the morning. The way you can go outside when the snow stops falling and, at any other time, it would be too dark to see ten feet in front of you without a street lamp or flashlight, but during that momentary break from snowfall, it's as bright as when the sun has just barely begun to look at your part of the world. The way that when you walk outside and there's no sound and no footprints aside from your own, you feel peaceful and completely alone, like you're the last person on Earth. That's how I feel right now, looking at the traffic light and all the perfectly white Everything around it. Only in that bad way this time. In a, "heavy fucking pressure on my chest and I want to cry and stop feeling so fucking alone all the goddamned time" way.

The wind and snow have slowed down a lot, so everything is less staticky and much clearer. The undisturbed, thick, white blanket outside makes me feel calm for the first time in at least a year, but this loneliness is still suffocating. I smile and think of going down the road to the park for some fresh air before it starts snowing maniacally again, but decide to take a shorter walk to the kitchen instead.

I open a cupboard that doesn't close all the way due to the amount of coffee and tea that's always crammed into it and grab a packet of instant coffee. I heat a mug full of water on the stove and then walk back to the window, slowly pouring the packet of coffee into the steaming water. I look over at a clock on an end table and see it's only 3:41 am. I'm not even surprised anymore when I think it's a certain time and it's always earlier than what I think. I'm always wrong about everything else. The nights seem to be getting longer and longer. It feels like someone has slowed down time and stretched out the black silk of night just to fuck with me.

The snow has started falling again since I came back to the window, but it's only slight flurries. I realize I need a cigarette. Sipping the coffee, I walk over to a worn-out recliner that I had draped my coat over the back of. With my free hand, I search all the pockets for our last pack, even though I already know which pocket it's in. When I finally get the pack out of the inside pocket, I find only two left, which is good, because my best friend can have one when he wakes up. I take another sip of coffee before setting the mug on a coaster lying on the broken coffee table and replacing it with a little white lighter.

With my cigarette between two fingers, I place the second one next to the clock on a little red notebook with a torn piece of paper that reads: "When you wake up, read. Try not to be too mad at me." I put on my coat, step outside onto the balcony, and light my cigarette with already shivering hands. The heat in my lungs feels good in contrast to the cold that licks my face and hands. With the cold, fresh air, I feel better and happier than I have lately and smile again. I look back into the apartment and hope my friend doesn't end up in any trouble, even though I tried my best to write everything out and explain it the best I could in the little notebook. I wouldn't want to put any more stress on him, or anyone else for that matter. As I inhale the last few puffs of tobacco and nicotine, I look over the railing of our sixth-floor balcony at the frozen, snow covered concrete below and think that, if everything goes according to plan, everyone will be much, much better off. I flick the finished cigarette far away from me and watch the sparks fly off with the wind. I think of how ugly the frozen concrete will soon look with its great red stain.

(I jump.)

(I land on the ground, head first.)

(I feel and hear my own neck and spine crack.)

(SNAP.)

(Stars and static swallow everything for the last time.)

(My ghosts cry blood and then vanish.)

....

SLEEP.

THUNDER.

THUNDER.

The lightning's static has pierced my fingertips while I slept. The robed creatures are starting to leave my bedroom, but I still feel as though I am under the sea, black and deep. With the waves above us. I call out: "WAIT: Was it all a dream? What did all of that mean?" The robed creatures turn and reply with a thousand and two and three-

quarter voices:

"NOTHING."
"NOTHING."
"Nothing."
"Nothing."
"nothing."
"nothi

....

GHOST SPEAK

CHAPTER1

A shapeless fog rolls through the trees, whispering, "Come to me, come to me, come to me." A shapeless fog rolls through the trees, I whisper, "Calm me, calm me, calm me." Electrical currents caress dead, sunken cheeks and the trees scream. There are hunters in the trees. There are hunters in the fog. There are haunters in the trees. There are haunters in the fog. They whisper, "Come to us, and we will end it all for you."
"I don't know."
"I don't know."
"I don't know."
"It doesn't matter at the end of everything."
A shapeless fog whispers, "You are nothing, to anyone or anything." I whisper back, "This is one that I do know." A shapeless fog creeps up, creeps around.

...

Cold winds push me. Coax the car to the shoulder. Towards concrete. Towards forgiveness. Towards my name: Forgotten. Here is my body, frozen like ghost's breath. Sitting in the middle of a dark and empty room, crying without tears. I control nothing, but who am I, or we, or I to control anything. There are lost trees inside me and every single one of them is dying. I want to die. Rusty spine in rotted flesh. Rusty spine in rotted flesh. Rusty spine in rotted flesh. Rusty spine in rotted flesh. Rusty spine in rotted flesh. Rusty spine in rotted flesh. Rusty spine in rotted flesh. Rusty spine in rotted flesh. Rusty spine in rotted flesh. Rusty spine in rotted flesh. Rusty spine in rotted flesh. Rusty spine in rotted flesh. Rusty spine in rotted flesh. Rusty spine in rotted flesh. Rusty spine in rotted flesh. Rusty spine in rotted flesh.

...

  Someone help me get this dirt out of my throat... In the morning, when I haven't slept... And in the morning, in the light that hurts my head... I'll still want to die. I'll still be alone. I'll still want to die. I'll still feel alone. And in the morning, I'll want to die more.

...

  Someone is talking outside. Someone is tapping metal against metal outside. There is no one outside. It's goes on and on. The tapping gets faster. The talking gets faster. There is no one outside. There is

no one outside. There is no one outside.
There is no one outside. There is no one
outside. There is no one outside. There is no
one outside. There is no one outside. There
is no one outside. There is no one outside.
There is no one outside. There is no one
outside. There is no one outside. There is no
one outside. There is no one outside. There
is no one outside. There is no one outside.
There is no one outside. There is no one
outside. There is no one outside. There is no
one outside. There is no one outside. There
is no one outside. There is no one outside.
There is no one outside, but the fog creeps
in. The ghosts ride it's back and breathe ice
into my spine. Screams.

...

*"Telephone wires
scream too."*

...

      The face of a man(?) Long, black
hair. The face underneath, one second
human but with sunken, black eyes. The
next second, a featureless triangular shape,
under the mess of hair. Switching back and
forth. Switching back and forth. Switching
back and forth. Switching back and forth.

Always. A voice and it screams, "Heavy, heavy, heavy."

...

...

Ripping roots. Everything dark and grey. My future's grey. Is yours? Is ours? My future is grey. My future is grey. My future is grey. My future is grey. My future is grey. My future is grey. My future is grey. My future is grey. Everything is blurry. Who cares about anything? Do you? Do we? Do I? Everything is blurry. The fog rolls in and screams. The ghost ride in and scream. Hunters scream. Haunters scream.

...

I am not worthy of you, but my future is grey and blurry. You won't deal with me for very much longer. Everything is blurry. The fog rolls in and screams. The ghosts ride in and scream. Hunters scream. Haunters scream, and I feel alone. No feeling around me, but I feel something, alone. No connection to or with anyone else, just drifting through an outside world trying to make it back home. Alone. Just a tether that keeps everything blurry and grey, and that's all think about. Alone.

...

A shapeless fog rolls through the trees, whispering, "Come to me, come to me, come to me." The forest of suicides screams, "Come to us, come to us, come to us!" They are beating me until I become one of them, because they know I'm already one of them just breathing failure.

...

Maybe if I could change into a new person every few days or weeks, you'd want me near.

...

"Do you want to die? Come to us, come to us, come to us."
"If it makes me feel less guilty for who, what, how I am, then please."

...

"Maybe I'm just nothing."
"Don't act like you haven't known that all along. Stop saying maybe in front of truths, it doesn't make sense. You are nothing."
"I am nothing."
"You are nothing."
"I am nothing."
"You are nothing."
"I am nothing."
"You are nothing."
"I am nothing."
"You are nothing."
"I am nothing. I am nothing. I am nothing. I am nothing. I am nothing. I am nothing."

...

I go outside and see groups of people. I don't know you, but you beg me to kill you. You may not look at me or speak to me, but something inside you does. To fill your throats with dirt. To fill your throats with blood. To take my knife, thrust it into your throats, rip out everything inside. Cut open your stomachs and lay all your insides out on the floor in front of us. Every time, I come a little closer to doing it. Come a little closer to being a screaming hunter. To being a screaming haunter. To having my own shapeless fog wrap around all of you and suffocate.

...

"Do you want to die? Come to us, come to us, come to us."
"If it makes me feel less guilty for who, what, how I am, then please."

...

Electrical currents caress dead, sunken cheeks and the trees scream. There are hunters in the trees. There are hunters in the fog. There are haunters in the trees. There are haunters in the fog. They whisper, "Come to us, and we will end it all for you."

...

"Are they talking to me or am I talking to you?"

...

I am not exciting, nor am I new enough for you. Not good enough for you. Less good for myself.

CHAPTER 2

There are few things better

    Than rain…

    Than lightening that lights up the entire night…

    Than thunder that rattles windows like bombs going off.

CHAPTER 3

Sometimes when the magnets
Switch the poles,
And the lows come in
Like heavy, anvil waves,
It's like hitting a wall
At a too fast speed.
The bricks fall hard
But don't kill me.
They just lay on me
And sink me down
And I can't breathe.
I'm drowning in thick,
Black water,
But staying alive.
It hurts and
I want the weight to finish
      Crushing me.
No one should ever feel like
It's because of them.
It's always happened
And it
   Always will.
Until it finally gets
What it's always come for
And the weights get taken for good.

CHAPTER 4

There's this great thing about manic depression: It's like you're in this repeating scene of being on a ship. There's calm seas and clear skies for a few days, or weeks, or a month. One night, the stars disappear suddenly behind big, black clouds and waves come crashing in from all around. Big, life-crushing waves and small, insignificant waves that come so fast that sometimes you can't tell the difference between the two. Eventually, one wave, big or small (at some point it doesn't matter because they all feel the same), hits the ship and you fall overboard. You sink underwater and it catches you by such surprise that the amount of breath you're holding in is small, small, small. The pressure from the water crushes down on your chest and you panic. Someone in the audience yells, 'Don't worry, the storm always ends.'

Yeah, the storm always ends. They always do, but when you're sinking the only thing that matters is that you can't tell which way is up. Everything is dark and foamy, and that little bit of air is shriveling and where the fuck is up. It isn't ever a question of, 'Is this storm going to end?' It's a question of, 'Is this little bit of air going to last me until the storm ends? Am I going to be able to find the way up before the ocean swallows me up?' Every time the scene closes, you find your way up and the storm ends and there's another moment of calm.

It goes on like this for years.

But at some point, the scene will have to stop repeating. The bottom of the ship will crack your skull, or your lungs will collapse, and you'll breathe the ocean in. The storm will end but you won't have made it to the top this time. When you finally do float up, your back is to the sky and your body is bloated and bluegreengrey. The roll of film burns, no chance of restoration. The theater lights come back up. No one leaves the theater because they all walked out before the end.

...

"Leaves, rotting on the ground, have more worth."

CHAPTER 5

Sometimes, I feel as though I have no one I can talk to, so I just write all this garbage down. I'm in the dark, but it's not a comforting dark. It's a dark filled with paranoia. No one can talk to me either. I'm fucking alone. Everything has been blurry. Everything has felt heavier. My want of dying is getting in the way of things again. I can't work. I can't sleep. I can't concentrate. I can't trust. It's my fault and it's not. This rears its head and kicks me in the chest, and I let it. What's the point of talking if I can't talk to just you? What's the point of motivation if I'm just going to die? What's the point of wanting to stop feeling so alone when it's never, ever going away? What's the point of writing this if no one is going to read it or understand if they do?

...

    I want to jump into a hole. Cover myself in mud and leaves. Push dirt into my ears so I stop hearing ghosts. Push dirt into my throat so I never say anything again. Set myself on fire and die lost in a forest. Set myself on fire and die lost in a forest. Set myself on fire and die lost in a forest. Set myself on fire and die lost in a forest. Set myself on fire and die lost in a forest. Set myself on fire and die lost in a forest. Set myself on fire and die lost in a forest. Set myself on fire and die lost in a forest. Set myself on fire and die lost in a forest. I want

to jump into a hole. Cover myself in mud
and leaves. Push dirt into my ears so I stop
hearing ghosts. Push dirt into my throat so I
never say anything again. Set myself on fire
and die lost in a forest.

...

    I hate all of this. I hate myself for
feeling so alone. I hate everyone around me
for making me feel so alone.

...

"Stop whining. You're fucking pathetic.
You're fucking pathetic. You're fucking
pathetic. Pathetic. Pathetic. Pathetic.
Useless waste of everything."
"I know. Please help me. Please kill me."
"Do it yourself. Pathetic crybaby."

...

    A life in the dark. Something close to
a life, but lesser than, in the dark.

...

    Ghosts keep screaming. Fog keep
whispering. The forest keeps calling. Ghost

keep screaming. I'm stuck and I don't which way is away.

...

A deep low again. I've shrunk to the size of a gnat and everyone around is too busy whispering secrets to notice I've disappeared.

CHAPTER6

The sky gets dark and crumbly. Static shoots and rumbles. Walls get thinner, and things appear.

...

Last night, I woke up to find I was already awake, doing something I had no interest in doing.

...

This morning, while driving, I dreamt that this truck changed lanes without seeing me. I let go of the wheel and let it crush me. I shouted goodbye to no one, and no one replied with the sound of crushed metal, glass, and bone. When I came back, I cried because it felt so good to leave.

...

"Why are you like this?"
"I don't know, but wouldn't it be funny if I never found out why I am, or who we are?"
"Christ with a leper nailed to your back, a hypocrite nailed to your front. Monsters nailed to your limbs and ribs. Worthless as roadkill, just a stain of meat and blood on the road of everyone around you."

CHAPTER 7

I started

taking pills

again.

CHAPTER8

In the blink
Of an eye,
A shadow appeared,
Said goodnight,
And stole your skin.

> *Someone ripped holes*
> *In the air*
> *And now they all*
> *Let themselves in.*
> *Creeping into worlds,*
> *Unnoticed by most.*
> *Wait until things start to fold*
> *In front of…*

Wind blows the curtains open. A voice screeches, like an old door opening.
"Coming…"
"Coming…"

"Coming…"
"Coming…"
"Coming…"
"Coming…"
"Coming…"

> *We're always near.*
> *Always coming closer.*
> *Ha. Ha. Aha. Ha.*

Are you Ghosts
Or Shadows?
Have you found out yet?
What Am I?
Ghost or Shadow?

> *There are no forests here.*
> *There are only haunters here.*
> *There are only the screamers here.*

What have I become,
If not Ghost or Shadow?

CHAPTER 9

XXXXXXX   This is black gardens. What happens here is whatever is perceived as XX real. Not you or I, but the actions we do. There is no time, however, there is a ticking clock. The clock is only used to settle one's nerves. The voices are warped, yes, but not when you come here as a sleeping soul. Sleeping soul hear my words clearly, as they are meant to be heard. If you are awake, my words will appear to be soft hushes of noises trying desperately to lull your soul back to sleep. But that is merely how I speak. What you are readi ng may appear to have mea ning, but only to your awake ned mind. If you watch closely, my n's are broken here, but not when you sleep. When you sleep, the letter n flows like a liquid form of silk, flowing through your nerve endings, much like a pixel. This is merely an introduction, one smeared with red ink from an old typewriter, sent through many fields of light and sounds. To put it into words you can hear would be to put it to words you don't understand while you are awake. So, for now, I bid you goodbye, until you fall asleep and I can talk to you in a golden voice. Goodnight.

....

    There is coffee spilt on your brand-new black carpet. It leaves a red stain. Your maid, whose name you've never bothered to learn, will never clean it. X (Sorry, I had to flip my record.) You are the only one who can X see the stain, which is getting bigger with every CLACK, CLACK, CLACK, CLACK, CLACK, CLACK, CLACK, CLACK, CLA-- of the typewriter in the next room over. (DIN

G)   You never even noticed the typewriter until I mentioned it. Investigate. You pass tattered chairs and end tables, slowly quickening with each step that leads you to the next room. But you stop... Hand on the doorknob. Turn door knob. Open door. Step past door..............

....

    Step past the door. The room enter is not a room, but the dense forest outside. The sounds of typewriters is no longer around you, only a distant memory, floating in the dark air of a moonless night. What you hear now are crickets. Water. Leaves. Owls. All night sounds have to offer are dreams, but you already knew this. The night creeps into your faint coat, and a whimper escapes, but not from you. Your shadow, it's his whimper. A cough. A sneeze. Th e owl tells you he's trying to sleep, but you're already asleep, so you don't understand the question. Why? The answer is tattooed on a tree, so which one? Where? He comes alone, unlike you. He is pure white. He is white with the evil of growing coffee stains. The sounds of harsh winds have never waken you before, why should they start now?/? There is a beggar below him, never asking for cheap change. He only asks the you follow the river. He points to a tree. On the tree is the word 'XXXXXX' and an arrow pointing to a direction you never learned in school. The tells you with a toothy grin to follow him through the yers and the iourtants. They all laugh at your face.

…….

Have you heard Mantoysheksa yet? He's quite wonderful, even if you don't believe in that sort of thing.

(AHEM)

Where was I? Ooohh,,, yyyeeesss......

The song bird, beggar, arrow, tree, "XXXXXX", and stain all laugh at you. This is a nightmare, but only because you allowed it to be. You never had to listen to my directions, you only did because I was the only one telling you to go anywhere. So, I shall continue.

Right past the arrow you walk. You follow the map you have wished for, the shadow and stain following so dearly and closely. But y u watch. There is black space all around you, imitating the rushing river. But you can see it, forget jasdfg, you follow her. Numbers follow as well. Big, vibrantly colored letters they are. Follow Shakespeare, don't follow you. Giants with long, flowing hair stand guard along the river as you approach it. The water is red. Stained white, but red and purple. The accordion player falls into a player accordion. Confusion. Jaksemof. ;/,#. Lies.

Your name is number and it's being called out from the loudspeaker in a crowded waiting room. A lie, she calls. You awake.

Or not.

However, it is time cigarette. Wouldn't you agree ?

....

CHAPTER10

Once I had a dream that you
Were a bicycle and I was,

Was the dusty dirt road.
And you tore up my face for miles,
Tore up my face for miles.
Ferociously slicing the indifferent molecules
Between yourself and a stream you found
Much more pleasing.

> *It's streaming, streaming.*
>
> *It's streaming, streaming.*
>
> *It's dreaming, dreaming of screaming.*
>
> *It's streaming, streaming.*
>
> *It's streaming, streaming.*

If I shed off all my skin
And let my muscles rot off in the sun
For all the bugs and the pointy teeth
Animals to eat,
Would you play the drums with my bones?
Play the drums with my bones?
Play the drums with my bones?
Play the drums with my bones?

> *It's streaming, streaming.*

It's streaming, streaming.

It's streaming, streaming.

It's dreaming, dreaming of screaming.

It's streaming, streaming.

It's streaming, streaming.

If I cut off the top of my head
And someone removed my brain,
Would you dust off your pretty feet and toes?
And toes.
And toes.
Step inside my head
And beat my ear drums,
Like how you play the drums.
So your skills can forever be
Embedded in my head.

It's streaming, streaming.

It's streaming, streaming.

It's dreaming, dreaming.

It's streaming, streaming.

It's streaming, streaming.

It's streaming, streaming.

It's dreaming of coming home to you.

It's streaming, it's dreaming, it's screaming.

It's streaming, streaming.

CHAPTER11

Someone is talking of keys and holes, but not keyholes. I tattooed them on my wrists, but I don't know what they are for yet. The voice is muffle, and only those bits come through. There's a vague sense of knowing I'm supposed to be doing something, but I don't know what it is. Why am I scared? Why am I scared? I know why I'm confused, but why am I scared?

....

Soft knocking on the outside wall, is someone trying to get in? Is someone just bored?

………

Who keeps waking me up? The voice is unfamiliar.

…….

"Ha ha."

"They are forgetting all about you."

The scream at me. The trees. The hunters. The Fog. At least they don't forget about me.

"But what if we do?"
(in a chorus of screams and whispers.)
"But what if we do?"

They scream at me. The trees. The hunters. The haunters. The fog. They do sometimes, for a few minutes or a few days. Not for long. This one is long. At least they come back. Can they see me because I'm like them? Can I hear them because we share the same voices? Ghosts and fog are different. Ghosts and trees are different. Not by much, but enough to make it hard to know who we are. Enough to keep me or us from knowing where we are. I know generally where I am, but we're lost. We're very lost.

"And forgotten, don't forget about that."

Words form promises? Such things don't, I don't think. Words are broke en to begin with, so wouldn't promis es? Screech in my ears? No, whisper. Maybe scream. But only in this ghost speak. Speak. Speak. Speak, hunters. Don't you know hot to become unlost? Help us/me/us. Us? Me? Is there a difference? I can't tell. I can't tell where I am, if I'm here or outside my body but seeing my hands slip through my body like water. Words flow out sometimes. Sometimes stuck. Sometimes there's too many trees, or hunters, or haunters. I'm scared.

"I'm scared"

"Scared of what?"

"Scared of everything. My chest hurts because my ribs are grinding their fronts together. I'm scared of losing my job because I'm lost and sometimes I just wander around and hear no one but the fog telling me I'll never be unlost."

"Like right now."

A shapeless fog rolls through the trees of me, whispering, *'You'll never be unlost.'*

....

- \Manic\ -

- /depressive/ -

- \Manic\ -

- /depressive/ -

- \Manic\ -

- /depressive/ -

- \Manic\ -

- /depressive/ -
- \Manic\ -
- /depressive/ -
- \Manic\ -
- /depressive/ -
- \Manic\ -
- /depressive/ -

"Until you die."

"Lost until we die?"

"Yes."

"Ha ha."

".ah aH"

…….

~~OKAY.~~

CHAPTER12

I am trying to lie on a tiny piece of wood in the middle of the ocean. I am lost. My body is cramped and uncomfortable. I am lost. No one is looking for me. I am lost. No one will ever look for me. I am lost. The wood is rotting and so is my flesh. I am lost. The ocean is dark and thick, or crumpled and ragged. I can't breathe. Far away from being unlost now.

".ah aH."

....

Sometimes their words come as thoughts, but incoherent and fragmented, like a radio going in and out and in and out and in and out and in and out and in and out and i n and o ut.

....

Last night, I saw the one talking to me. I saw the form he chose for me. He didn't speak but turned on a flashlight. We went through a seemingly infinite number of hallways until I passed out and/or fell asleep. I don't know where we were going. I think a shadow stole my skin.

....

CHAPTER 13

I was diagnosed with schizoaffective bipolar type disorder, instead of just "bipolar".

Hahahahaha.

A shapeless fog rolls through the trees, whispering, "We have you now." A shapeless fog rolls through the trees, I whisper, "What is there to have, really?" Electrical currents caress dead, sunken cheeks and the trees scream. There are hunters in the trees. There are hunters in the fog. There are haunters in the trees. There are haunters in the fog. They whisper, "We have you now."

      Sometimes, I find pieces of myself, scattered around the house. The pieces don't fit back in the empty holes though. Should I throw them away or throw them into a box? What is becoming of me? Who am I? Does anyone else care that things fall out of me? Does anyone else care to know where I know I'm headed?

Suicide.

Is there an end that isn't the end?

Suicide.

Is there a way out?

Suicide.

      Attacks in public. Now everyone knows I can't handle my brain. Attacks in public. Admission of suicidal thoughts. Attack in public. Attack in public. Attack in public. Attack in public. Attack in public.

Attack in public. Rain covers me. Shadows cover me. Cloaks to hide from and to be hidden from.

CHAPTER 14

All the new wounds circle crimson air.
Crimson air circles the ground.
The forest is on fire.
Ashes sting my nostrils

And the crimson air soaks my eyes.
Go slowly,
I'm out of my mind.
The forest is on fire.

Are the haunters okay?

Are the hunters okay?

Are the ghosts okay?

I hear them all scream.
I hear them all whisper.
Through the crimson air,
The fire is fake.

"Or is it?"

The forest is on fire though.

"Or it's not."

I cannot tell who's there.
Just a presence.
And a sound.
The sound of a forest on fire.
The sound of a person standing behind me.
The sound of breath.
The sound of being watched,
Through the crimson air.
Face to face with a mirror.
No reflection,

Just crimson air and shadows.
A fire blooms,
But there's no heat anywhere.

CHAPTER15

They swallow static like rotten fruit, following me around. Blood rushes to my fingers and they go numb. Fear. Finders have come. The shadows have voices of static, and they swallow the static around them. There is static all around us. They sing in static, they breathe out static, and swallow it back in. The finders lead the hunters and haunters behind the shadows. Charcoal breaks and smears on my fingers. It gets in my mouth and I cough out static bile to be swallowed by the mass of shadows. There are keys on my hands but nowhere to run. Nothing to lock or unlock. Are my hands smearing charcoal or shadow?

Screams.

Having found something, I creep. Like a feather, the crimson air floats around me. The shadows drift around me. The static gets thick and then thin, pulsing, pulsing, pulsing. It matches my heartbeat. Whatever I found is stolen by a Finder. It leaves a charcoal streak across my arm and there's blood, but the finder is just thick air. Like a ghost, crying out with static breathe and charcoal blood. The haunters are near. The hunters are near. The ghosts are near. The forest is dense. The forest whispers and everything else screams. The keys on my hands itch.

Screams.

I walk over static hills, but I don't know where I'm going. The air is filled with static and the sky is covered in it. Is the whole world surrounded by static? Is the static everything?

Possibly.

Where are the Watchers?

CHAPTER 16

Velvet strings tied around my wrists cut into them and I bleed. It feels like soft blood. The shadows are still marching around me, vomiting static and breathing it all back in. I'm tied to a dying tree and the middle of a dying field. The border of the field is on fire and the smoke covers the dark static sky. I choke on ash and cough out more charcoal.

The shadows dance. Behind them, I can see the hunters, dragging their bloodied knees on the grown, faces distorted. The haunters float above them, screaming. The tree whispers to me. I can't understand it, and it shakes with fear of the flames and of its soon death.

    Fire but the fire is cold, freezing. Static breath, ragged, escapes my nostrils. My hands are still numb, and the keys still itch. The velvet loosens, and I blink.

    I'm in a white room, a l o n e.

Alone?

CHAPTER17

Blackened red eyes.
Falling out of trees.
Coming out of the ground.
Shadows everywhere.
The crimson air mixes with the charcoal on my hands,
Everything gets muddy red.
They can hear me breathing.
I'm hidden, but they can hear me.
The velvet strings are still around my wrists.
This tree groans.
It whispers suicide.
The shadows whisper suicide.

The haunters scream,
"Let us take you, let us take you!"
I want to go,
I want to hide.
I want to hide,
I want to go.

CHAPTER18

In the dark,
They creep towards me.
The problem is suicide
Or something similar.
Some want to help,
Some want suicide.
It's hard to tell
The difference.
There is a cave,
Cold, dark, and lonely.
A portal to somewhere else.
I enter.

I'm surrounded by concrete.
It's a giant room,
Empty,
Save for a pillar in the middle.

A giant rabbit
Peeks around the pillar.
I ask it to show me
The way.
It nods,
And walks towards a door
That has suddenly appeared.
The rabbit takes me
Through a massive
Concrete maze.

I fall asleep before we reach the end.

There are stars everywhere,
They align with Jupiter.
A kiss for a shadow.
Follow them through a hole.
Use my hand keys.
The doors unlock.
I fall asleep.

I wake up in a white room,
A L O N E.

Alone?

A black mass squeezes
Out of a corner.
It comes toward me.
I fall asleep.

A blanket of snow.
A tree that shivers
And whispers.
I'm in the tree.
It whispers

Suicide.

It whispers

Suicide.

My fingertips go numb.
I fall asleep.

Ghosts scream.
Haunters scream.
Hunters scream

Follow them?
Please tell me:
Follow them
Or are they following me?

There are dark trees,
Mangled and black.
The whisper stories
Of suicide.
It is a forest full of them.
The whisper on the same note.
The shadows live in them.
The haunters live in them.

The hunters live in the.
The ghosts live in them.
Everything's dark and shaded,
Green and thick leaves,
Black and burnt wood.

Ritual.
Ambient.
It makes sense to me.
It's what I do.
It's what I've done.
Release things with song.
Ritual.
Ambient.

(Say something, don't keep me alone.)
Finders find me.
And hold my hand,
Leaving their charcoal skin
On mine.

In the dark,
They creep towards me.
This cave is cold,
But the trees are warm,
Like they're still burning
On the inside.

I can't focus on what
I'm supposed to.

CHAPTER 19

In a dream, I was no longer lonely. I dreamt the people around me were no longer offended by my loneliness.

"How can you be lonely when you're around people? How can you feel alone? It's not right, you shouldn't be like this."

None of these words were said to me. I could hear deep, soft notes begin to tear through my body and my head, and I woke. I woke weeping because I was sucked back into loneliness. I woke weeping for the one thing I knew I'd never have.

I wake, and then fall back into the black of the dream. Fall slowly in a swirling black, I jerk, but stay asleep. It's the only way to keep the ghosts away. They speak, and I weep it the dream. I weep because I know I can never fully keep them away.

Stay asleep and see it. I only want to stay asleep and see it. It's the only thing that keeps me alive. I see it, and it glows. I don't know what it is, but it glows brighter than any light I've ever seen. And then it disappears. I run down concrete steps, making slippery sounds. I run: Run, run, run, run, run, run, run……………………

I slipped but I wanted to keep running. Shadows follow me as I slip down the stairs. They try to slit my throat. I want them to, but I want to catch the thing first. All I see is the orange-black of a city landscape, trying to see where all the throat cutters are. All I see are the concrete steps, slipping, slipping. Slipping. Falling. Slipping. Falling. Slipping. Falling. Slipping. Falling, Slipping. Falling. Slipping. Falling. Slipping. Falling.

"Please keep away", I scream at the Shadows. "Please keep away. Please keep away. Please keep away."

The Shadows will suffocate me. I want to get away from the, but they won't leave me be. I just want the light, nut the Shadows are closing in. They are trying to suffocate me and slit my horrible throat. My throat will open wider than any canyon, unless I can get to the thing. "Please want me back. Please want me back. Please come to me."

All I want to do is die. I want to die if I can't have it and the loneliness stays. It calls out, but I don't know if it wants me back. It calls out in a forlorn voice and I call back. I call back with voiceless words. The words are filled with airless, voiceless breath. The breathless, airless voice fills the words with worthless nothing and every word sounds like a worthless nothing. The thing that I want, will it ever want me? Will it never know how much I want it? I scribble down the voiceless words, but they just look like an empty, blank, worthless page. The empty page crinkles and ends up in the trash. The actual words fall onto my chin, watery and tasteless. I try to grab the watery words with cold hands, but they slip through my numb fingers. As the words fall through my fingers, my fingers crumble painlessly. They crumble into tasteless dust. They never reach it, they never reach the thing I want. I think someone is keeping my watery, tasteless words. But I don't know. But I do think. And it's true. The Shadows are keeping the thing from knowing what my stupid, worthless words are. They are keeping me from getting to it.

    I am drying in this terrifying dream. I no longer feel calm with the missing feeling of loneliness. The Shadows are succeeding, and I'll be dead soon. I'll be dead soon. I'll be dead soon. I'll be dead soon. I'll be dead soon. I'll be dead soon. I'll be dead soon and I'll never get to let the thing know that I want it. It will never know exactly what my watery, tasteless, worthless words sound like, and I weep. I weep because the thing will never know exactly what I want to say or how I feel towards it.

      I will die soon. I will die soon. I will die soon. I'll be dead, and the thing I want but will never have, will never miss me. It will never miss me because it will never hear my worthless fucking words.

      The thing will never know me. I am grasping at nothing because it will only ever know nothing. It will never know these tasteless, watery words. It sits next to me and still knows nothing, still does not know I exist for it. See it and know nothing will ever compare. It will never know about me because its ears are normal and cannot hear worthless nothings.

      It sings, and I can't understand the meaningful words. But it doesn't matter, because the thing will never understand mine either. And I start to fade into blackness, another segment of the dream realm. The new dream is just as shitty and I fucking hate this. All I want is to dream, to not feel loneliness or death breathing down my back, but then I hate all of my dreams, because this thing still doesn't know me. It still can't hear me. I still can't make my voice unwatery, unvoiceless, unworthless, undead. "Please kill me." "Please kill me." "Please kill me and get this hell over with." "Please."

And the soft deep notes are still playing. Through each dream, I can hear them, and there's more black around me than there was before, and I'm still bleeding to death.

My hair falls out. My flesh rots off. My throat gapes like the mouth of a goblin shark, ready to kill me, but I'm so close to death, it doesn't matter.

A dark mist surrounds me, with soft and deep notes guiding it and I don't know where I am anymore. I don't know who I am anymore.

I wanted to hold something in my hands to me what or who I am. A mirror painted black. A charred map. The picture of the thing in my coat pocket catches on fire. I leave it there to burn me. I feel loneliness. Again. The photograph burns through my ribs and starts to chew away at everything inside of me. It doesn't hurt as much as I would have thought. It just feels like loneliness. I weep. I weep because the photograph was the only thing I had of the thing I want and now it's gone. Again, I have nothing to keep me from being lifted out of the mist, out of this dream.

I'm in a house, I can see stars. They burn bright and hurt my burnt, rotting flesh. The fall into me and make me warm for the first time since joining this dream. I'm as warm as a fever. Trying to keep as much sickly, sweet blood flowing from my shriveled veins fastest. And the stars fall. The thing I want drifts farther away, I almost can't see it anymore. I run. I run until my lungs bleed and my feet cave in on themselves.

I fall. I fall on my knees, hard, and they bleed. The things yell back at me and I understand it for the first time, "I'm nothing to you. You're a fool. Stop chasing me. Leave me the fuck alone." I try to give up, but the things hooks are still lodged deep into my flesh. The faster it runs away, the harder the hooks pull on me. They pull me, and my face is pressed against the bloodied dirt beneath. The faces in the mist laugh are me, a goddamned fool.

I am pulled back into a kitchen. It's overflowing with black, smoke filled bodies, their gaping mouth screech and scream truth into my biggest fear, they scream in my ears, telling me the one thing I want will never, ever want me back. STOP. STOP. STOP. STOP. STOP. STOP. STOP. Everything they say is true, and the more their words (full of voices) stream at me in the horribly overcrowded kitchen, the more their words hold truth. They hold more meaning. They hold more devastation. The hold me destruction. They hold more of me. More. They hold more of me in the screeching, screaming, clutches of wordtruth. Thoughttruth. Feartruth. It gets stronger, and eventually, it shrivels me into nothing.

I am the nothing I was always meant to be and will never. Never. Never. Never. Never. Never. Never. Never. Wake up again.

CHAPTER20

Where are the haunters now?

Where are the ghosts now?
Where are the hunters now?
Where are the shadows now?

CHAPTER21

The dream stretched out
Like an ocean,
Glittering with moon-silvered waves.
There were stars
Littering the sky,
But there were no
Familiar constellations.
The ocean was pocked
By groups of tall black trees.
There was a ghost
Sitting where the beach
Met the water,
Where the water met its shadow.
It sat looking out at the trees.
I sat on an outcropping of rocks
Watching it.
It breathed so slowly.
sat on the black sand, staring out.
I wondered what it was thinking.
I wondered if ghosts thought at all.

CHAPTER22

A woman in a crimson cloak
Stands amid
The crimson air.
The air encircles her
As the ghosts
Clutch at her feet.

The shadows howl,
And she
Cringes.

The haunters
Fear
Her.

CHAPTER 23

None more black
Than a cloud of shadows,
Pushing it's way
Through
A forest of screaming trees.
Trying to find a way
Out of my head.

Storms collide.

CHAPTER 24

FINGERPRINTS OF SHADOWS

COVER THE WALLS.

CHAPTER 25

Anxiety over order.
A false face.
Shadows creep in here,
But straight lines lie outward.
Functioning:
They call it.
But barely.
Only barely.

CHAPTER 26

    Things repeat themselves:
A shapeless fog rolls through the trees,
whispering, "Come to me, come to me,
come to me." A shapeless fog rolls through
the trees, I whisper, "Calm me, calm me,
calm me." Electrical currents caress dead,
sunken cheeks and the trees scream. There
are hunters in the trees. There are hunters in
the fog. There are haunters in the trees.
There are haunters in the fog. They whisper,
"Come to us, and we will end it all for you."
    "I don't know."
        "I don't know."
            "I don't know."

"It doesn't matter at the end of everything."
A shapeless fog whispers, "You are nothing, to anyone or anything." I whisper back, "This is one that I do know." A shapeless fog creeps up, creeps around.

...

Cold winds push me. Coax the car to the shoulder. Towards concrete. Towards forgiveness. Towards my name: Forgotten. Here is my body, frozen like ghost's breath. Sitting in the middle of a dark and empty room, crying without tears. I control nothing, but who am I, or we, or I to control anything. There are lost trees inside me and every single one of them is dying. I want to die. Rusty spine in rotted flesh. Rusty spine in rotted flesh. Rusty spine in rotted flesh. Rusty spine in rotted flesh. Rusty spine in rotted flesh. Rusty spine in rotted flesh. Rusty spine in rotted flesh. Rusty spine in rotted flesh. Rusty spine in rotted flesh. Rusty spine in rotted flesh. Rusty spine in rotted flesh. Rusty spine in rotted flesh. Rusty spine in rotted flesh. Rusty spine in rotted flesh. Rusty spine in rotted flesh. Rusty spine in rotted flesh.

Finely crushed charcoal dust in my nose and on my fingers. Shadows stealing my skin. My skin turning black and charcoaled, learning to live burned. From here, I know nothing. I'm supposed to get it, but I don't. Stream of consciousness and the unbearable weights. Fuck. Fuck. Fuck. Fuck. Who am I?

Who am I? Who are you? I am nothing worth talking about. My insides are worth more than me. Everyone screams inside and my head splits. I hear them outside and I turn, looking foolish. Fuck. Fuck. Fuck. Fuck.

CHAPTER27

Stars look farther away. Why?

The world is an empty room and I'm alone.

The world is an empty room except for shadows

Ghosts

Haunters

Hunters

But mostly the shadows and I.

But, yet, I am alone in this room.

Isn't this what I wanted?

CHAPTER 28

The shadows cry out.

> *"Kill yourself. Kill yourself for us!"*

What happens if
I do?

CHAPTER 29

Find me before
I kill myself.
I have so much more to do,
But this urge is so strong…
These voices are so strong.

CHAPTER 30

In the end, I am Me. The shadows are me, the ghosts, the haunters, and the hunters. The suicide forests. All the screaming, moaning, whispering happens in me and so much around me. The shadows and whispering are around me, but it's still in me. How does one live with all this noise?

PART TWO

Poems

FUCK MY FRIENDS, AND PROBABLY

YOU TOO

Follow dulled senses.
Grasp at rotting twine.
How many friends
Really know what I do?
How many friends
Really care what I do?
Not many.
If that.
Follow numbed senses.
Grasp at rotting faces...
...Thank you all for being here.
Now I know I'll
Never be around more
Fake,
Two-faced,
Self-obsessed mother fuckers,
Than I am right now,
And I include myself…
Follow drugged senses.
Grasp at rotting flesh.
I swear this bridge
Was already burning
Before I ever got here.

SHE DID NOTHING WRONG (HARSH LAUGHTER RINGS OUT)

Do you still believe
You can keep familiar hands
At home,
While you let your
Hands and eyes and heart wander?
My words have truth,
Yours have ash, shame, and the
Fear of being caught
In the act of being
Not the helpless, tortured,
Innocent.
Keep friends as dense
As yourself who believe
Only ashen words,
So you're never told that you
Deserve to come home to
Sparkless emptiness.
Only that you deserve
Oh, so much better...
...Don't pretend to be a princess
When all you are
Is a cut-up,
Ugly,
Step-sister.

I AM A SADIST, I AM A HUMAN TORTURE DEVICE

I am the nonexistence of
Free Will.
I am a boa
Constrictor,
Constricting what little
Of your life I'm not squeezing
Out of you,
And you,
And you,
And mainly you.
I am a vise.
I am a dictator.
I am Glass the Impaler.
I am a life-long sentence
In a Judas Cradle.
I am the brazen bull with tubes,
So everyone
Can hear your
Blistered,
Tortured,
Screams.
I keep you in a cage
In the basement,
Away from everyone you know,
And you will never have friends.
"There are two sides
To every story."
But in this life,

There is only theirs.
There's nothing worse than me.

A MARTYR OF NOTHINGNESS

I was born:
Dark blue and unholy.
A spokesman for
An umbilical noose.
(My mother tried to hang me in the womb.)
A martyr of
Nothingness.
Born into absurdity.
From the beginning,
It was always there.
Waiting and lurking:
For me to notice how
Absurd it really all was.
It really all is.
It's really all there is.
Forced to live:
Dark blue and holy.
A miracle no one ever wanted to see.
Told only unholy.
Never the holy,
Or even the decent.
I was born dark blue and holy.
But only after
I learned how to give up.

MAYBE A ROPE OF SOME SORT

There is a string,
Or maybe a thread,
That pulls on something
Inside of me
While you are away.
The longer you are away,
The more that something
Gets pulled out of me.
So,
Please,
Don't stay away for too long.

THE VASTLY ROTTED FRUIT OF LIFE

You are
Dripping wet,
Like a melting stalactite.
You are forceful and manipulative.
And I whisper:
"Let my fruit
Bleed into your womb,
And then leave it to rot
In your stomach
Until I fail you completely,
Or incompletely,
And all of me rots

You to death."
And the cave grows darker still.

PLANTS

Before the seamstress comes
To take
All my sinews and tendrils,
I pray to her
To plant them
In some unborn child's mind.
Like a forest of suicides
Planted in hell.

GUARDIAN ANGEL

What is the point
Of a guardian angel?
What are they guarding?
Or are they just for show?
Little, flittering, shiny lights
That just make you
Feel good about your day.
Something for you to thank
For small things that are too big
For you to have accomplished
But

Are too small for a god
To have the time
To deal with.
Or maybe it's just
The support system
For people who have none.
If that's the case,
Why don't I have one?

MAYBE

Am I dreaming?
No.
Maybe.
"Does it matter?"
"You wouldn't ever remember
If you were."
Maybe.

BLURS AND SMUDGES

Can you touch me?
I can't feel,
My body's gone
Whiskey-numb.
Young, lost, schizoid, lost.
I can't feel my skin but

I can feel black smoke bodies
Creeping around.
Can they touch me?
Yes.
Their hands chill my skin,
I can tell by the way
My hair rises in the shape
Of a hand.
Their hands tug
At my clothes in public,
And I turn fast
Only to see a stranger
Staring wildly.
Can the strangers touch me?
They could
But they won't.
Only the black smoke bodies
Dare to touch
And chill
My whiskey-numb skin.
They say:
"Seeing is believing."
I only believe in
Blurs, smudges, and
Black smoke bodies.

SMUDGES AND BLURS

Can they keep away?
Yes.
But they wouldn't dare leave
My whiskey-numb skin
And dampened clothes alone.
Sometimes,
I sit and let
Black sand fill my flesh.
The sand gives me words
To place together haphazardly.
The sand gives me images
To place on paper in asymmetrical lines,
Full of dying ink.
Place numb hands
On frozen glass
And then burn,
Watch the body burn.
Watch my body burn.
Watch,
The black smoke bodies
Chill my flesh back to health.
The black sand keeps me
From remembering my dreams.

SO MUCH HOLD

I speak like I was born for nothing.
But the words only have
So much hold,
Because they are stolen
From your dreams.
And you've heard them all before.

PROPER

The only
Proper
Way to die
Is alone.
And if you die
Any other way,
You may as well
Not
Die
At
All.

UNTIL YOU MEET ME

Can't focus here.
Zone out.

Eyes bleed.
Suffocating.
Anxiety.
The feeling of being trapped
Like a dead rabbit in
A too small cage.
Won't notice if I'm gone.
Or notice too much.
Can't escape.
My skin burns.
Burning flesh smells sweet
In an acid snowfall.
Or is it ashes?
My own ashes, falling
On me from the future
While my past self
Burns alive.
My present body
Stays nonexistent.
Can't focus on moving away.
Can't focus here.
Ears bleed.
Eyes bleed.
Oil spills out of my mouth.
Lean forward and
Let it spill out onto red carpet.
Constant shakes.
Anxiety.
Suffocating.
Becoming a dead rabbit
In a too small, empty

Cage that smells of whiskey.
"There's nothing more worthless
Than a dead cat."
"Until you meet me."

SYNAPSES

Synapses misfire and I see
Static in front of me.
Synapses misfire
And the walls are covered
In static.
Synapses misfire and my
Ear drums burst.
Static flows into my brain
From the walls.
Splitting static headache.
Kill myself if I could,
But I can't see worth static blood.

NOW

You only ever exist
To a certain point.
The point of
A second.
Imagine now,

If you will,
How many points
Of existence
You've been in until now.
Until now
Until now.
Until now.
Until now.
Until now.
Until now.
Until now.

COULD YOU BE AN ADULT?

If you were placed
Inside of an adultsized room,
Could you be the adult
You needed to be?
Or would you stay
The childsized life
And make living in the
Adultsized
Room
Impossible?

SAME TIME

We lie alone.
On the same bed
At the same time,
We lay alone.
If I can't feel you,
You're not there.
If you can't feel me,
I'm not there.
We spend the night alone.
In the same bed
At the same time.
We drink alone,
In the same room
At the same time.
We talk out loud,
Alone.
We stay alone for years,
At the same address,
At the same time.

WARM/SUNNY

A tall, white horse
On top of a very
High ladder.
The weather is

Warm and sunny up there.
Away from torture devices
Here,
Littering the ground
Below her.

GREY/WET

How is the weather
Up atop your
High
High
Horse?
Is it bright and warm?
I hope if I
Ever get to ride
A horse as high
As yours,
It's grey and wet.

BLEEDING BRAIN

Empty, black casket.
Only filled with
Black, airy mist.
Stretching bi-polar.

Bleeding nose.
Bleeding mouth.
Blood on the bed.
My pillow.
My carpet.
My sink.
The tile in the bathroom.
Stained the floor of the shower.
All my white shirts.
Bleeding knuckles.
Bleeding forearms.
Bleeding throat,
Whether for "art", or not.
All because of a
Bleeding brain.

ALONE

I want to stay
In a locked room
Forever.
I want to be alone
Forever.

RROOTT

Listen,
Quickly,
To the heart beat.
Does it sound rotten to you?
It is, it is.
The heart has rotted.
I know you think
There is no heart at all.
But you can hear it now,
Pumping ash and dusts
Into your ears
And my purplish-black veins.
I have eradicated your
Disease,
And now the rotted pieces
Will flake away
Like skin cells
And I can breathe again.

EVERYTHING IS

Everything is
Dark and all consuming.
Crushed skulls and suffocation.
Lives are built and
Towns are burned.
Everything will be

All destroyed.
Father's life has proven
To be doomed
And Son's life will follow suit.
Everything ends in
Death,
Preferably soon and
Self-inflicted.

THE KNIFE

I am the knife between your ribs,
The thorn in your godlike side.
Someone to laugh about
When in the safety of friends.
The one to make your life
Look better than it ever actually
Could be.

DIG A HOLE IN YOUR BED

Will you dig a hole
In your bed and
Bury my books and bones?
You can use the dirt
To get the sleep
You've been dreaming of.

MAPS

Arms like maps.
Scars like roads.
Veins like dying streams.

THEY WON'T CARE

Is this the meaning of life?
To destroy yourself
In front of an apathetic audience
In a house that reeks
Of selfishness and booze.
To destroy yourself while watching
Desperate dicks twitching
At desperate cunts
With no courage to dispel
The desperation in either.
I can see fear
That you've chosen
Too apathetic an audience,
Too selfish an audience,
And when your destruction is finished,
They won't care.

BARREN

I am a springless autumn.
I am only a gift for Death,
But she has refused me before.
There are things
Worth coming and going for,
But not here.
A waste land is stood upon.
Stories don't tell how it came to be,
Only that it will
Never be anything more.
Who wants a barren, wasted gift?
Not you.
Not even Death.
Not even Death.
Not even Death.

FLUORESCENT

My eyes are burning
Like crowded loneliness
And your breath tastes
Like blood.
Fluorescent lights dim out.
Fluorescent radiation seeps in.
Our flesh slides off,
Our hearts fall out,
Our lives slip up the stream of radiation,

And the world is better for it.

UNFAMILIAR

Wake from a dream
Where you were in the same place,
Or did you wake in a dream
From where you were awake?
Why does none of it
Seem familiar if
It's all the same place?

IT ONLY GETS WORSE

I have stopped taking
My pills
And
If anything happens,
I'm sorry
To anyone who may feel
Hurt.
If you ever think
You've gotten better,
You haven't
And you never
Will.

USE/BLAME

You spent time with me
But you speak to me
With forked tongues
And drooling lungs.
I said I don't want to,
But you heard that means
Use them
And then blame them.

SELVES, Pt. 1

Kept alone on a beach.
Kept lost on a drained sea.
Kept all to my...
Alone...
We saw and never knew,
Words thrown and
The worst only heard.
Fog came in
But never left.
Fog comes in
And confuses even
The least alone.

Kept alone on a drained sea.
Kept alone in a beach.
Kept alone by

Myself,
Or yourself,
But very much alone.
Slept or unslept on sand
Next to warm flesh,
But felt only cold air.
Kept lost and by your...
Alone...

SELVES, Pt. 2

Sometime soon the fog
May lift
Enough.
Enough to see one another
In the distance,
Old but anew.

Sometime soon the fog
May lift
Enough.
Enough to touch one another
On the fingertips,
Warms up but still too far.

Sometime soon the fog
May lift
Enough.
Enough to place lips against ears,

And whisper,
'Hello, it's been so long,
But so sorely missed
And maybe even needed
But almost too long.'

Sometime soon the fog
May lift
Enough.
Enough to embrace one another
Instead of only our...
Alone...

SO SCARED

I am fearful
That you will lose interest
In me
Again.
I want you all to myself.
And if that's controlling
Or selfish,
I'm sorry.
You just fit my
Selfish,
Fragile
Frame
So perfectly.
I am so scared.

I am fearful
That you will give up on me again.
Please don't give up on me,
With my sunken skin
And sunken mind.
Please don't give up on me,
And my frozen tendencies.
Where I feel like I can't
Move or breathe or speak.
Please don't.
I'm so scared.
I'm so scared.
I'm so scared.

BROKEN OR BREAKING OR CRUMBLING AWAY

My voice is a wreck.
Broken.
Keeping everything else broken.
Stay quiet.
Stay quiet.
Stay quiet.
Stay quiet.
Stay quiet.
Stay quiet,
And still break more.

BASEBOARDS

Sometimes I will watch them
From the baseboards in their house.
They told me I should love you
And I think I've done okay so far.
I think.
I used to swear
On my father's grave.
I used to swear
At my mother's house.
Now I'm just swearing
That I don't want to live
But I kind of want to live
And it's all so confusing.
I've said it before
But I'm losing myself
In the sea of sound and bright lights
And I'm doing the best that I can
With the shriveled brain that I've got left.

VIOLENT

Father was violent and hit you.
Father was violent and made me touch him.
I don't trust,
I don't trust,

I don't trust anyone,
Because you never taught me how.

Family is worthless…
Family is the most worthless
Thing I have.

You'll die soon.
You'll die soon,
Without knowing me at all.
Without knowing your granddaughter.
You'll die alone.

How does it feel,
To have a family?
How does it feel,
To know
The last thing you said was:
"If you want die so bad,
Then just do it.
I never loved you
And you're not my child."

VOICES RISING

Voices rising,
Whispering.

DARK

It's dark.
The dead of night.
A world full of shadows.
A world full of ghosts
And the unwanted.
It's so dark.
The want is lost
Somewhere
In the fog of dark.
It's lost in its wants,
In its place,
In its conviction.
>What exactly does it want?
>Where exactly is it?
>How hard should the want keep trying?

It's dark here,
So fucking dark.
I watch the want
Slide around
On its hands and knees,
Grasping at its surroundings,
Trying to get a feel
Of where it is
And when it should head
To where it belongs.
>But it's so dark.

It's always so dark.
Shadows stand in circles around it,
Watching.
      I am the want and a shadow.
The shadows grow
In numbers every night.
      Is there a day?
When it's all dark,
It's hard to tell.
Whatever the case,
They grow in numbers.
They stand in a circle
And stare at the want.
They stare at me and
I stare at myself.
The ground is
Crumbly and rough.
The want is bleeding.
      Who's bleeding?
I am, and it's dark.
      Can anyone see it besides the
shadows and ghosts?
      Can anyone see me besides the
shadows and the ghosts?
      What is the want?
      What am I?

I fall down a path
Full of burs and thorns.

Ghosts follow,
Their ectoplasm ripping behind them.
The path is in a forest.
 It's the middle
Of a clouded night.
No moon,
No stars.
No light.
Just trees and bushes
And thorns
And suicide.
        What will become of me?
                Who will I become?
        What will I want?
        What will I do?
All of this in   a next life.
        How do I know I'll get one?
I keep falling,
Arms and hands
Covered in blood.
My clothes covered
In the burs and dirt.
        When will the spinning stop?
When I stop falling,
I'm in a clearing.
There's a ring
Of trees
And shadows with
A tree stump in the middle.

I stand on it and ask.
           "Who am I? What am I?"
    Silence.
Always silence in the dark.
Always dark in the silence.
The clearing is dark,
But I can see the shadows
Surround me.
They stare and wind
Whooshes through my ears.
       Is it just the wind or is it voices?
Sometimes it's hard to tell.

      Where to begin?
          Where to end?
I would lie naked
On these rocks forever.
A black beach with warm,
Black water rushing my feet.
Completely alone
With the sound of water.
No wind,
Just voices carried over thousands of miles.
Whispering incoherent words
To lull me to sleep.
The weight of depression
And anxiety,
All but gone.
An erection and

No one to touch it,
Just the water touching my feet
And the rocks touching my back.
Completely alone
With the sound of water.
I hope my words are read
In black and grey images.
Sounds drift in from a wormhole,
Somewhere outside of here.
There are people and
I'm not by myself there,
Only alone.
Here I am both
But it's not bothersome.
It's nice and quiet here.

I found pebbles on the beach
That make the wails of ghosts.
I get another erection
And it goes away.
No one around to notice,
No one around to care.
     Why should I care?
The sound of beach
Makes me lay down again,
Putting me to back to sleep
Alone.
     It's dark.

I'm in a thicket of rose bushes,
Thorns slicing my skin.
   What am I doing here?
     Why am I naked again?
Blood soaks the dirt below me
And I feel weak.
It's dark and all there is,
Are thorns in my skin.
Ghosts and shadows
Swoop between the branches
And poke the holes in my flesh.
I crawl towards
A flash of light
And fall into the clearing.
I lay on my back and bleed.
Gasps of air.
Dirt infests my skin
And stops the bleeding after a while.
The ghosts and shadows
Swoosh in circles around me,
Licking the blood off me.

I'm back on the beach,
Still bleeding.
The ocean waters
Wash over me and it burns.
The wormhole still makes sounds
From somewhere else,
But I'm in too much pain

To hear anything.
> Alone.
>> Again.
Covered in blood and ectoplasm.

Alone forever.
Alone forever.
Alone forever.
Surrounded and alone forever.

TAKING BLOOD

A chorus of voices.
A round of followings.
 In love,
There is nothing
But hurt.
Like the rose thorns
Through soft flesh.
Cutting and slicing you down
To a puddle of blood.
I sit on a tree stump,
Covered in blood.
Naked and crying.
The ghosts and shadows
Continue poking cold fingers
Into my wounds,

Flying in a grey circle,
Taking turns
Taking blood.
The clearing gets darker
And darker.
> Where is the soft beach with its warm stones and water? Why am I stuck on thorns in a clearing in the woods?

Another wormhole forms
And I can hear myself
Surrounded by people,
But alone.
I feel as alone
As if I were bleeding
On a tree stump.

The moon turns black.
The ocean turns cold.

A room, dark and grey.
Figures surround me in cloaks.
They raise their hands above me,
And I can see through them
To the empty walls behind them.
An empty bed except for me,
But there's heat coming
From the other side,
Like a body was there before.

The figures lower their hands
And the room goes black.

The bed is in the middle
Of the ocean
And I'm naked again.
The salt water prunes my skin.
The sheets are soaked and heavy,
But the heat is still there.
        Where is this other body?
I crawl into the water
And my feet touch the bottom.
Something slashes my Achilles heel
And I start to drown.

I touch my hard cock
And it evaporates.

My lungs are almost full of water now.

March on to the beat
Of something less than me.
Ghosts prick my fingertips.
Shadows blacken my eyes.
Razorblades slide through the air
And caress my skin.
Soft blood drains
And I would bleed for you.
Crumbled earth and rotten fire.

                I would bleed for you.
I am isolated from everything,
Everyone.
I will watch myself
On the other side of a glass pane.
Underwater,
I will drown.
I will keep myself in a cage
Until one day,
I come and slit my own throat.
                I would bleed for you.
I will take my own life,
Because it's the only one I can.
I don't want to live anymore.
                I would bleed for you.
                    I would bleed for
anyone if I die.

I hope I die.
I'm lost.
                I would bleed for you.

Black roots grow
From the ceiling
And suffocate me,
Wrapping around my throat
And diving into my mouth.
I want to be anyone else.

I scream for help,
But no sound escapes.
I writhe,
But my limbs won't move.
I wake up,
And I still can't move
Or shout.
I fall back asleep,
Wake up,
Fall asleep,
Wake up,
Fall asleep,
Wake up.
                I would bleed for you if I could move.

Everything comes around
Like nothing in view.
Something carries me away
And I float.
I float on my bed
In the middle of
The ocean,
Naked and cold.
Disintegrating and cold.
I watch waves roll towards
A black beach,
But the bed doesn't move closer.

Concrete on the ground,
Concrete in my skull.
A blessed fall from a high building.
The want is crawling away,
Who knows where?
There's blood on the ground,
Following it,
Coming from it.
What will happen when
The want bleeds to death?

In a dream,
I was wanting to die.
I crawled through the kitchen
With blood smearing the floor.
I was tired of being alone.
I want nothing more than to be alone.
Please speak.

ALWAYS CREEPING

In come ghosts,
Out come shadows.
Always creeping.
Always creeping.
Always creeping.

Take me away
Ye ghosts and shadows
Take me,
I don't belong here.
I am a burden.
I am a burden,
I am a burden.

A black talisman of death
Rips through my throat.
Your necklace burns your chest,
And you don't even feel it.
It's taking your soul away.
Taking your soul away.
Taking your soul away.

In come ghosts,
Out come shadows.
Always creeping.
Always creeping.
Always creeping.

I am hollowed out,
Full of emotions
But emotionless.
Craving fear.
Craving fear.
Craving fear.

Ghosts tend to my fear.
Shadows tend to my fear.
Ghosts tend to my fear.
Shadows tend to my fear.
Ghosts tend to my fear.
Shadows tend to my fear.

In bed,
I'm awake.
Ghosts keep me awake,
And I'll never be the one
Who sleep by your side.
And in the morning light,
I'll dream of white light,
Engulfing me.
But it's the ghosts.
But it's the ghosts.

My brain goes so fast,
But it's ghosts the keep it.
I'll amuse myself with thoughts of anything.
I'll panic myself with thoughts of anything.
But it's the ghosts.
But it's the ghosts.
But it's the ghosts.

I'm drowning from the flesh in my head.
Another sound comes through like hot lead.
Finding out I'm alone in my bed.

The sound carries well,
But it gets buried beneath it all.
Time to slip and once again I fall,
Into a dreamless sleep
Filled with roots in my mouth
And around my throat.
The roof comes crashing down
And awake just to fall back in,
Into the dreamer's deep sound.
        Am I awake?
                Am I awake?
                       Am I awake?
Am I awake or is it something else?

SPLIT SECOND

There is this fear
That surrounds me,
Dark and heavy.
I am alone in this.
There may be others
Who have felt this fear,
But they were alone it as well.
It's an isolating fear
And nothing penetrates.
Nothing gets through.
Just darkness and weight,

Enough of both to crush you.

> It gets so heavy.
> It gets so heavy.
> It gets so heavy.

I watch the flesh slide from my hands
And my feet.
Every minute that passes
Is agony.

Drink.
No one would touch
Your cock anyways.
Shut up.

The calm before the storm,
That split second between
Mania and depression.
That split second between
Depression and mania.

ISOLATION

Somewhere,
Deep in a vein
Is a found collage.

It bleeds like me,
And I bleed like it.
Full of black
And white
And grey ink.
It supposes and breathes.
Isolated in the vein,
Never coming out,
Never showing its face.
Further and further it goes.
Backing up against a wall
And hiding behind
Books to hide its face.

Somewhere,
Deep in a vein
Is a found collage.
I find it and we stay
Isolated together.
Thick walls between us.
No more photographs,
Please.
Leave me alone.

Leave me alone.

Leave me alone.
                    Leave me a lone.

              L e a v e m e a l o n
              e.

Let us rot together, alone.

Everything stops sometimes.
I feel like I'm
The only one moving.
Sometimes,
I'm the one who has
Stopped,
And everything else
Goes by incredibly fast.

I can see a shadow
Through the window.
It looks and smiles at me.
It's whispering something,
But I can't hear it
Through the glass.
I want to know what it's saying.
        I want to know what it's saying.
              I want to know what it's
     saying.
It knocks on the window,
But it's soundless,
Like the sound gets
Swallowed up in its
Inky black hole skin.

I'm shaking.
I bled yesterday,
And the shadow can smell it.
It wants more,
And I want to give it more.

I write slowly
Because I'm shaking.
The shadow laughs silently
At my shaking.
My stomach is
Empty except
For coffee.
I'm shaking,
And the shadow keeps laughing its mute laugh.
Jazz plays on speakers
Somewhere near
And the shadow
Scratches at the windowpane.
The sound is still swallowed up
By its black hole skin.
I don't know what's worse:
The shadow itself
Or the fact that no sound escapes
Through the window pane.

I've been watching you.

I hear a voice in my head.

I've been watching you.
I've been watching you.
I've been watching you.
You're not doing so well,
are you?

No, no I'm not.
But you know this.
All you shadows know this.
I'll bleed for you if you want.
I'll bleed for you if that's what you want.

You'll bleed for us.
You'll bleed for us.
You'll bleed for us.
You'll bleed for us.
You'll bleed for us.
You'll bleed for us.
You'll bleed for us.
You'll bleed for us.
You'll bleed for us.
You'll bleed for us.
You'll bleed for us.
You'll bleed for us.
You'll bleed for us.
You'll bleed for us.
You'll bleed for us.

You'll bleed for us.
You'll bleed for us.
You'll bleed for us.
You'll bleed for us.
You'll bleed for us.
You'll bleed for us.
You'll bleed for us.
You'll bleed for us.
You'll bleed for us.
You'll bleed for us.
You'll bleed for us.
You'll bleed for us.
You'll bleed for us.

<u>DEAD OF NIGHT</u>

They come for me
In the dead of night.
Black enough to see
In the dead of night.
Surrounding me,
In the dead of night.
Latching onto my throat,
In the dead of night.
They keep me awake,
In the dead of night.
Inky black holes,

In the dead of night.
Suffocating me,
In the dead of night.
Latching onto my feet,
In the dead of night.
They keep me awake,
In the dead of night.
In the dead of night.
In the dead of night.
In my bed at night.
In my bed at night.

In a dark room,
I cannot breathe.
I cannot scream.
In this night,
Roots grow out of the ceiling
And enter my throat
Through my gaping mouth.
I cannot breathe.
I cannot scream.
Devoid of good.
I am lost.
I cannot breathe.
I cannot scream.
In the dead of night,
My breath is taken from me.

My blood has coagulated,

And I cannot breathe.
I am atrophied,
And I cannot breathe.
In the dead of night,
I am awake
And I cannot scream.

In the dead of night,
They come.
My Father comes and stands in the corner of the room.
He's come for the past six months.
Always at the right corner of the bed.
Staring with black eyes.
In the dead of night.
He doesn't move.
He doesn't breathe.
He doesn't blink.
In the dead of night.
Staring.

Staring.
Staring.
Staring.

He watches
In the dead of night.
I don't know what he wants.
Maybe he's supposed to

Help me with something.
Maybe he wants something from me.
Maybe he's not dead.
Maybe he's alive somewhere,
And his body can leave
But unable to move.

Stupid.
He's dead.

What does he want?
In the dead of night.
After all this time,
Why did he decide to start
Watching me now?
        Why can't he move?
        Why can't he talk?
Is his tongue cut out
For some crime he committed
While alive?
Does he even know where he is?
Does he even know it's me
That he's staring at
In the dead of night?
In the dead of night.
In the dead of night.
Maybe he's a warning.

A warning of what?

Why do you talk to me?
                Who are you?

No one.
No one.

You must be someone.
Someone who knows something.
Find it out.
The rabbit never leads me
Through the maze.
The man in the suit never visits anymore.
You say you are no one.

In the dead of night.
In the dead of night.
In the dead of night.
In the dead of night.
In the dead of night.
In the dead of night.
In the dead of night.

Why the dead of night?
Why must the night die?
How does it die while I'm still awake?
Am I ever awake?
I'm just a dream,
In the dead of night.'

I don't know.
We laugh at you for not knowing.
But we know nothing as well.

That doesn't help.
That doesn't help.
That doesn't help.
 Sacrilege in the house of me.
In the house of us.
In the dead of night.,
You crawl from the shadows.
In the dead of day,
You come from the shadows.
I must isolate myself.
        I must isolate myself.
                I must isolate myself.

What good would the do?
We'd still find you.
Your father will still find you.

Then tell me what it means.
Tell me what the dead of night is.
Tell me what the dead of night is.
Tell me.

We will see.
Maybe soon.

Maybe never.

IT LIFTS ME

In these times,
I'm carried away
By the ocean.
   It lifts me
And carries me
In the dead of night,
In isolation.
     Isolated
From the world
That is cruel.
     Isolated
From the people
Who are cruel
And talk
Too much.
The ocean is
A bed.
The night is always dead.
Find a way
Home.
Find a way
Home.
Find a way

Home.

ACTING LIKE AN ADULT

It's time to start
Acting like an adult.
Do you hear me?
I am no exception.
Are you throwing rocks through windows?
Are you still burning through bridges?
Do you hear me?
I am no exception.
I'm forgiving
But I'm not forgetting.
Sometimes a rock slips
But I'm doing my best.

I was a burden,
I know this now.
And I still play the victim
Sometimes,
But so, do you.
So, do you.
So, do you.

SPLINTERS

There are splinters from
Flowers grown of decay.
And fragrant
Despite the corpse
They grow from.
The flowers are red and white
And smell sweet
Like honey.
The corpse is my own,
Fallen in melting snow.
Fallen in hunger and loneliness.

And I would have died anyways
If given half the chance.
I would have died anyways
If given half the chance.

I was your servant
And you threw me away
Like the empty shell I am.
The flowers grow so
Bright and so
Sweet.
So, unlike me.
So, unlike me.

So, unlike me.

But I would have died anyways
If given half the chance.
I would have died anyways
If given half the chance.

Frailty.
Oh,
The frailty.
My rotten hands clasped
Around a stone,
Poised to throw.

FARTHER AWAY

Farther away it seems
I go from myself.
I could see myself in the mirror
But from the other side of it.
My body's not mine,
               Oh hahahaha,
My body's not mine.
Where is the line
Drawn when everything

Feels so far away?
When it feels like my
Body is inches away from where
I'm standing still?
Farther away it seems
I go from myself.
I could see
Through my own hands.
So unnatural.
So unnatural.
Farther away it seems
From myself.

FLOWING AWAY

Flow away.
This is precious time.
This is precious blood.
Flowing like the Mississippi.
And my lover is waiting,
For health,
For words,
For help.
But time is flowing away.
But blood is flowing away.
No way to hold either
In your hands,

With the cracks and spaces
And fragile,
Rotting skin.

And my lover's eyes
Are weary with tears.
A stream.
A river.
A lake.
An ocean,
Full of salt and blood.

Will I drown?
Will you drown?

ROADKILL

These shadows are
So unnatural.
They creep around
And haunt like specters.
They don't want to be seen.
And me,
I am dead leaves,
Blown around directionless.

I'll never be a specter,
Despite being away
From my own body.
I am quiet and let myself be blown.

Can you feel me try
To creep up your bones
Like I want you to creep up mine?
Or,
Am I a specter,
Unnatural and without feeling?
Lost in the wind
Of the air conditioner,
Untouching you.
Lost in the blankets
And sheets
And untouching.
Shepard me towards your bones.
Shepard me towards your bones.
Shepard me towards your cold bones
And warm marrow.
Takes these sheets off
And leave the path
Unpocked and clear.
But I am quiet
And let myself be blown away
By the air conditioner.
Let myself disappear
Into sheets

And blankets
And the mattress.

The shadows stare
                    (staring, staring,
              staring, staring)
At me the whole time.
They live in the corners
Of the room.
Creeping and wanting to be unseen,
But I can see them.
I can see them.
Why can I see them?

While I was broken,
They took advantage of me.
Now I scream,
"Why have you taken my sanity?"

"Why would you want it?"

"Because everyone else does."

As the rain falls,
The shadows stand outside,
The water dripping through them.
Unwet, undry.
Help me get by,
Have faith in me

That I will never be anything.
I will never be anything
But dead in the road.
Roadkill, unsightly.
Roadkill, unwanted.
Roadkill, unloved.

UNDERLINE

UNHEARD

In turbulent times,
The monsters come through
And suck the air from my lungs.
I am always frozen in fear,
My screams come out as breathy gasps,
Unheard.
Unheard.
Unheard.

"Salvation is ever farther away, how will you deal?"
"Your father killed himself, how will you live?"
"You are your father's child, no matter how much you may wish against it."

In turbulent times,
I cry.

Breathy gasps.
Unheard.
Un heard.
Unheard.

DISINTEGRATE

Memories.
Moans of pleasure
Causing heat on thighs.
Oh,
How I wish it were happening now.
Happening always.
Touch me until I disintegrate
Into you.
Touch you until you evaporate
Onto me.
Lay my head on your chest.
Let me feel your life.

SWEET DREAMS

Sleep, come now
But you won't
Without the pills.

Find me here,
Waiting
With open arms.

Turn away,
Don't
Turn away.
I need you
Now
More than ever.

Sweet dreams,
Come to me.
Sweet dreams,
Come to me.

I'M A GHOST

I tried to find
My way in life,
But I can't.
I'm lost
Here.

Because I'm a ghost.
Because I'm a ghost.
Because I'm a ghost.

DON'T YOU SEE

A pillow sinks
Into a bed.
Panic sets in
And I can't rest
At all.
Don't you see what's happening here?
Don't you see what's happening here?
Don't you see what's happening here?

Panic rises
And
Panic rests.
Panic rises
And
Panic rests.

In the night,
I'm in a fog.
In the night,
I'm lost again.
Words and pictures
Roll through my head,
And I can't rest.
Don't you see what's happening here?
Don't you see what's happening here?
Don't you see what's happening here?

Panic rises
And
Panic rests.
Panic rises
And
Panic rests.

But I never do.

HIDDEN

Something is hiding.
Something is keeping quiet.
Forever hidden.
Forever hidden.
Keep your eyes closed.

They'll come after you,
Like they come after me.
I must stay hidden,
But they always find me.
They always find me.
They always find me.

SHINING EYES

Something in the dark
Creeps towards me.
      Am I dead?
      Am I asleep?
Aware of shining eyes,
Focusing on me,
Panic rises.
Never hurt before now.

I AM CRUSHED BY MY OWN WEIGHT

For forever
I am nothing,
Just a burden.
Coming through the woodwork
To ruin everything.
For forever
I am nothing.
Just a burden.
Forever sinking,
Never floating.
I am a weight of concrete
Taking me to the bottom
Of the sea.
A victim,

Played out.
Who am I really?
What am I really?
A loose tendril,
A concrete weight,
And burden
On all who encounter me.
There are things that must be discussed.
Things from the past
That get brought up for no reason
And debilitate me.
I am crushed
By my own weight
And worthlessness.
I am crushed
By my own weight
And worthlessness.
I am crushed by my own worthlessness.
For forever,
I am a dead animal.

AT TIMES

At times,
I am lost
And alone.
I feel dead.

At times,
I want to be dead,
But I want to stay alive.
It's a conundrum
I've yet to figure out.

IS ANYTHING WORKING

      I keep to myself.
I don't like to talk.
I want to be alone.
I want to be left alone.
My head hurts and my stomach is empty.
I want to be left alone.
There are voices keeping me awake.
I take pills,
But are they still working?
I listen to music to drown them out,
But is it working?

WHERE

In the night,
My breath is swallowed
By roots
And my father.
Shadows creep around the bed,
Waiting to take me.
      Where?
I don't know.
(Maybe somewhere better, somewhere cleaner, somewhere nicer, somewhere less stressful.)
I don't know.
I don't know.
Maybe somewhere worse.

There's an opening
Near me.
It follows me.
An opening to
Another dimension.
And it follows me.
The shadows creep
Out of it.
It lets them come out
And follow me.

There's an opening

And it smells like brimstone.
I know it's there,
But do they know
That I know?

The shadows grab
At me.
I think I've said it before.
I think I've said all
Of this before.
There's a river
Carrying them through the opening.
        What am I doing here?
        What am I doing here?
        What am I doing here?
        What am I doing here?

I AM NOTHING

In this world,
I am nothing.

KEEP IT TOGETHER

Creeping out of windows,
They fall in line
For an attack.
They wait until I'm asleep,
And then sit on my chest,
Pulling at my throat tendrils.
Raving to each other
About how I will die.

Keep it together.
Keep it together.
THERE'S A CLOUD

There's a cloud,
It's grey and black.
It looms over me
And never goes away.

WHAT

Something happens.
     What?
You don't know.
     What?

Something happens.

I WANT/I NEED

I want to meet
The man in the suit.
I need to meet
The man in the suit.
I want to meet
The man in the suit.
I need to meet
The man in the suit.

CONFUSION

Are the voices
Here to help?
Are the voices
Here to make things worse?
There is so much
                       confusion.

FUCK

FUCK.
FUCK.
FUCK.
FUCK.
FUCK.
FUCK.
FUCK.
FUCK.
FUCK.
FUCK.
FUCK.

CRUSHED

On the side of the road,
Animals lay
Littered.
Organs
Splattered.
Blood
Splattered.
Bones
Crushed.

MY MIND IS CLUTTERED

My mind is cluttered.
How do I
Free it up?

SHIT

SHIT.
SHIT.
SHIT.
SHIT.
SHIT.
SHIT.
SHIT.
SHIT.
SHIT.
SHIT.
SHIT.

DREAMS, Pt. 1

In dreams,
I'm floating
In a white room.

There's a giant rabbit
That leads me through
A maze.
In dreams,
I'm floating.

DREAMS, Pt. 2

A dream,
From a red room.
A dream,
From a white room.
Something gives way,
And worry creeps in.
Anxiety rears its head
And I fall on the ground.
My chest throbs
And my hands shake.
I remember dust,
Dirt,
Rust.
A red door.
Crying.
Trembling.
Worry creeps in
And I can't control my body.
I can't control anything.

KEEP ME WARM

In a cold room,
The shadows
Shrink back.
But worry stays,
More so even.
I am a brittle leaf,
Hanging on for dear life
At the beginning of winter.
A cold rain falls,
And I dangle there,
Shivering and staring at shadows.
      (staring, staring, staring, staring.)
Keep me safe.
Keep me warm.
Keep me safe.
Keep me warm.
Keep me safe.
Keep me warm.
My fingers are frozen.
The worry is heavy enough
To make this
Little leaf drop.

GREY FACES

Grey faces
Calling out
In the middle of the night.
Grey faces
Calling out
To me in my dreams.
Grey faces
Calling out
To me in waking.

Muffled voices,
Muffled words.
Calling out,
Calling out.

Grey faces
Peering through windows.
Grey faces
Watching from across the road.
Grey faces
Whispering in my ear.
Grey faces
Tugging at my shirt.
Grey faces
Hiding things.

Muffled voices,
Muffled words.
Calling out,
Calling out.

Grey faces
Keeping watch.
Grey faces
Listening.
Grey faces
Stalking.
Grey faces.
Grey faces.
Grey faces.

Muffled voices,
Muffled words.
Calling out,
Calling out.

THE ART

This was one
Of the most chaotic times,
The forested hills,
And vendettas of
The great families were conducted
By skilled swordsmen recruits
Of a dissolving
Hereditary aristocracy.
Some individuals
Took vigorous expectation
To the moral standards
Of the times.
Boredom was banished,
Teams of dancing girls,
Musicians,
Acrobats,
Lay in the kitchens.
Despite chronic disorder,
The traders and merchants
Made fat profits.
Several thousand crimes
Were punishable
By death or mutilation.
They were sawn in half,
Boiled,
Or torn apart by chariots.
The words were identical

In that they merely
Made use of the word's
'Peace' and 'war'.
The words were identical
In that they merely
Made use of the word's
'Peace' and 'war'.
The words were identical
In that they merely
Made use of the word's
'Peace' and 'war'.
The words were identical
In that they merely
Made use of the word's
'Peace' and 'war'.
But most men
Of the later age
Realized that peregrinations
Devoted
To the promotion of pacific
And ethical objectives
Were a waste of time.
The author of "*The Art*"
Was one of these men,
And even though he
Did not in fact find
A patron,
He must somewhere
Have found a preceptive ear.

Otherwise his words
Would have died as
Did those of most of
His fewer original
Contemporaries.

In "*The Art*",
It speaks of witches
And how most are part
Of a coven,
When most are single witches.
An athame in his hand,
Slicing his palm,
Letting blood spill onto a waxy blank page.
The "*Art*" becomes
Something else entirely.
"*The Art*" becomes isolation.
Isolation.
Isolation.
In its isolation,
One can only believe
That it is one's own
Isolation and not some other's.
I do not know
Why that is,
But it amounts to
Schizophrenia.
Something outside
Of yourself that digs

Into your soul,
Eating away at
Yourself and keeping you
From knowing what is real.
Multiple personalities
Exist within "*The Art*",
And within me.
      How many personalities do you have?
      Is better to have multiple or just the one?
      Which one makes for a superior being?
      Which one makes for a lesser being, something to be locked away and fed pills?
The witches know
About the isolation
That comes in waves.
They know that the
Personalities will never go away,
No matter what device
Is laid upon them.
This is just that,
A story of
Schizophrenia,
Like all stories laid down
Before this one.
      What is a stream of words but the word vomit of someone else's personalities?

I understand that
Schizophrenia and multiple personalities
Are different diseases,
But at what point do they join?
    Do they ever join, or is it my
imagination?
Some say schizophrenia,
The voices,
Are a gift from God.
I don't believe in God,
So whom are they a gift from?
    Are they even a gift?
They tell me what
Words to put down
And how to arrange them,
But sometimes they talk
All at once and
Everything ends up
Incomprehensible and confusing.
    Is this confusing?
    An odd way to start or end a book?
    Am I supposed to acknowledge that
this is even a book?
The pages are black this time.
Someone told me to do that,
Someone who doesn't
Exist beyond myself.
Someone who doesn't
Exist to anyone else,

Except for maybe now
That it's on paper.
    Fuck.
    Too many voices at once, I don't
know who to listen to. Why are the pages
black this time?
    Fuck.
    Fuck.
    Fuck.
    Fuck.
    Fuck it.

*"YOU ARE THE WORST HUMAN
IMAGINABLE."
I AM THE WORST HUMAN IMAGINABLE.
FUCK YOU.*

Printed in Great Britain
by Amazon